JOURNEY

—— OF ——

SECRETS

Pam Fish

JOURNEY
— OF —
SECRETS

PAM FRIOLI

author
ready

For information contact Pam Frioli
authorpamfrioli@gmail
authorpamfrioli.com

Published by:
Author Ready

Copy Editor: Kim Autrey
Content Editor: Debbie Ihler Rasmussen

Cover design by Kirsten Capunay
Interior book design by Francine Platt, Eden Graphics, Inc.

Paperback ISBN 978-1-958626-38-2
Ebook ISBN 978-1-958626-39-9

Library of Congress Number: 2023907014

Manufactured in the United States of America

First Edition

Dedicated to My Mom
Leila Champ

CHAPTER ONE

It's time. I'm turning fifty this year. Who knows how it'll end: happy, sad, undecided. It's a scary black hole I'm wandering into. A place where I can see the entrance, but not the exit. My perceptions about my life, my past, maybe even my future, are at stake. Once I know the truth, I can't go back. My hopes and dreams are based on the reactions of a total stranger.

How strong *are* blood ties? Powerful enough to bring us together? *I'm* willing to face the facts, but is she? Did I wait too long to find out? I don't even know if she's still alive.

I paced around the room.

The most crippling question of all, Will she want to meet me?

What if she says no? How do I move past the pain? She doesn't even know me. If she refuses, I'll be devastated.

I can't let my thoughts go there. I'm beginning the adventure of a lifetime. Now's the time to buckle my seatbelt, enjoy the ride, and pray.

God already has it worked out, one way or another.

CHAPTER TWO

My name is Patrish, and I'm an adoptee. Have you ever asked yourself how far you'd go to find the truth? To me, the truth matters. But will it leave me free? Or heartbroken?

I was fortunate enough to be adopted and raised by two wonderful parents. My dad passed in 1992, my mom lives close by and supports me one hundred percent.

In 1989, I requested information from an adoption agency and received a non-identifying info sheet. It contained the only information I've ever found about my birth parents.

My hands trembled while I held the info sheet. I had worn the corners ragged from searching its contents over the years.

I bit my lip as I read it again. My birth mother's description sounded a lot like me. Blonde hair, blue eyes, and freckles. I clutched the paper to my chest. Do I look like her? It seemed highly probable.

My birth father also had blue eyes and dark blonde hair. Their ages surprised me. I was born when she was twenty-six, and he was twenty-eight. I imagined them much younger.

The papers indicated she wanted me to have the advantages of a two-parent family. So, where did my birth father fit into all of this? I wondered how many other family members I had out there. Did my birth mother ever think about me? Could she love me?

Like so many times before, tears filled my eyes.

I sighed. The same questions had plagued me for years.

My adoption was private, and the records in California were sealed. I doubt in 1955, anyone could have imagined the role computers would play in discovering valuable information. I'm sure my birth mother never expected me to track her whereabouts. I hope she's ready for this because I'm starting with her.

Deep, cleansing breath. Tonight, I'll start with prayer. For me, it's the best place to get an understanding of the possibilities that lie ahead. I pray I can accept the answers I find, no matter what, whether good or bad.

I pray for understanding from my family as I begin this emotional journey, and for a thankful heart. I don't have to do this on my own. God is always by my side, and I know He only wants the best for me.

CHAPTER THREE

It was a cold and drizzly Monday morning, February 28, 2005. I wasn't going to let the weather dampen my spirits, so I put on my reading glasses and clenched my jaw with determination. I picked up the non-identifying info sheet and sat down at the computer.

Brent came up behind me and put his hands on my shoulders.

"Adoptee. Good place to begin. I'm glad you're starting this process. You've wondered about her for a long time."

I took a deep breath and blew it out slowly. "Yep, here we go."

I'm not internet savvy and have no idea how to begin this process. I decided to type in the word *adoptee*. This one word brought up dozens of sites. Support groups, rights to know articles, and registries connecting birth parents and adoptees, as well as companies featuring internet searches.

I clicked on several sites, comparing the different services they offered. I decided to take a closer look at a company called Fact Finders. They specialized in California adoptions and boasted a 97 percent success rate in finding birth parents.

It sounded good to me, so I closed my eyes, voiced a silent prayer, and clicked on the icon to request a quote.

My sixteen-year-old daughter, Hayley, called from the next room. "Mom, don't forget we need to get to school."

I'd been so absorbed with research, I forgot what time it was.

Thirteen-year-old Nate came into the den. "Dad, are you taking us to school today? Mom, I can't find my backpack."

"Sorry, bud, not today. I have a meeting."

I shook my head. *Teenagers. A statement and a question without taking a breath.* I answered Nate, "By the door to the garage. Get in the car, and I'll be there in a minute, after I say goodbye to Dad."

I stood and stepped into Brent's warm embrace.

"You've got this," he said. "No matter where it leads, we support you."

After dropping the kids at school, I came back to the computer. The site wanted any information I had collected about my adoption. All I had was a copy of my altered birth certificate, the non-identifying info sheet, and one court document.

I always knew I had been adopted. My parents, Linnea and Jerry Campbell, had adopted me and my three siblings as infants, and they told us we were adopted at an early age. Through the years, I looked but could find no information about my birth parents.

My brother Blake, even at twelve, proved to be a better detective. One day when I was fifteen, he burst into my room grinning.

"Hey, look what I found."

Annoyed at the interruption, I snapped, "You getting into trouble again, little brother?"

Unfazed, he laughed. "No, you'll thank me for this," and handed me two official-looking documents.

I grabbed the papers from his hand. "I hope I don't have to bail you out again. Trouble follows you everywhere."

I stopped short.

Wide eyed, I realized he had an official copy of my adoption. *Baby girl Donovan* appeared at the top, followed by my birth name. *Diana Donovan.*

My voice squeaked. "You big snoop. Where did you find these?"

He wiggled his eyebrows. "In the file cabinet in the back of Dad's closet." He held up another paper. "My first name was David. I have Lindsay and Josh's papers, too. I don't think I'll show them, though. They'll rat me out."

I smiled and touched his arm. "Good work, Blake, but you'd better put them back. You know Dad wouldn't want you going through his files."

Years later, Mom gave each of us our papers.

I had the document Blake had given me when we were kids, and I wondered if I should include another piece of information I'd found years ago.

In 1995, I made a phone call to someone who researched California adoptions. I remember my stomach jumping as I dialed the phone number.

"May I speak to Nancy Hart?"

"This is she."

"Hi, my name is Patrish Fagiano. Sue Harvey gave me your name. She told me you helped her find her birth mother."

"Yes, I do provide that service."

"Can you explain how it works? I'd like to get information and possibly search for my birth mom."

"Were you born in California?"

"Yes, in San Diego."

"Okay, we can go to the California birth registry. When were you born?"

"November 5, 1955." My head was throbbing.

I heard papers rustling. "Hang on a minute, let me find the file. Do you know what hospital?"

"No, my altered birth certificate doesn't have it," I stammered.

"No problem. Here we go. Looks like your mother's maiden name is Long, or it could be a married name. This information isn't very clear. I might have a difficult time getting the details."

I wiped my hands on my pants and gulped. "What do you mean by difficult?"

"I usually see a clear path when I find the name. I don't see one with this name. Mixed up records, incorrect names, married or not married. It isn't precise."

Shaking my head, I shifted in my seat. "I'm not ready to start right now. Maybe in the future."

"It's okay. Give me a call if you change your mind."

I never tried again until now.

I added the two names to the form, Donovan and Long. I didn't know the significance of either name. Would these names be enough to help me find her? I faxed the copy of the official adoption document, rechecked the form I'd filled out, and pressed the click here for a quote button.

In a return email, they stated that the review period would be two business days and thanked me for the opportunity to work with them.

Early in the evening, another email came through. I held my breath.

> We believe we can positively identify and locate your biological mother. We're happy to say we typically get it completed in two-to-five business days after you authorize our services. The fee is $750 but will not be charged until the search is complete. You will receive her full name, address, and phone number.

I let out a high-pitched squeal. "Brent, you've got to see this. They say they can find her."

He hurried into the room and read the email over my shoulder.

"This could be it. You could be face-to-face with her or at least on a phone call soon. Hallelujah. This is what you've prayed for."

I rubbed the back of my neck, closing my eyes to stop the dizziness.

"I can't believe this. Within days, I could know all about her, meet her." I frowned. "What do you think about the fee they charge? Is it too high?"

Brent bent down and looked straight into my pleading eyes. "It is high, but this is too good to pass up. Go for it."

I took his face in my hands, pausing to rein in my emotions. "Thank you. Your encouragement means the world to me."

Brent kissed my forehead.

I turned back to the computer and hit the reply and authorize button.

Now, we wait.

~~~~~~

That evening, I decided it'd be a good idea to keep a journal. This journey marked a momentous occasion.

Feb 28, 2005

Today it begins. I finally got the nerve to look into finding my birth mother. The internet connected me to an agency specializing in CA adoptions. I'm scared and excited. Where will this lead? The cost is a little high, but Brent agrees it's time to move forward. The company said they complete searches in two-to-five days. Wow. Will it be that easy? Here I go.

CHAPTER FOUR

I sat straight up in bed when the alarm clock blared early the next morning. My thoughts jumped to Fact Finders and what new information would come my way. Ever the optimist, I slipped out of bed. My feet made soft impressions on the carpet as I hurried to the computer in the den and turned it on.

Had they already begun the search? Would I find anything out today? I held my hands over my pounding heart.

One email from Fact Finders. I took a shaky breath.

> We need one more thing from you. Please send us your complete contact information. We keep it confidential.

I shook my head. *Just a request.* I sent off the information they needed and received a return email.

> If all goes well, we'll have your case completed in one-or-two days; we will call you to obtain your payment info and to release the results to you. About twenty-four hours later, we'll email your receipt and research report.

I smiled at how quick they were to respond and knew from now on, I'd check my emails all day, hoping to hear from them. The computer screen pulled me like a magnet, sucking me into cyberspace and linking me to my past.

Before the end of the day, another message came. I gasped out loud, slapping my hands against my cheeks. Every muscle in my body tensed up as I shouted, "Hayley, Hayley! Come here and look at this."

She came running out of her room, wide eyes, and mouth open in surprise at my urgency.

I pointed to the computer screen. "Read this and tell me I'm not dreaming."

Reading it, she grabbed my arm. Leaning in close, a grin spread over her face to match mine. We locked our eyes for a moment, then returned our gaze to the screen, reading the words again.

> We are not 100 percent certain, but we do believe we may have located your birth mother. We'll need to make a phone call to her to verify the facts. I can assure you we'll be professional and discreet. Do we have your permission to make contact? This will open the door for you. We also need to know what your expectations are. Are you seeking medical history? A relationship? Please explain your position a little more, so we know how to present you to the woman we believe is your birth mother. If you have any questions or concerns, let us know immediately. If you approve of us making contact, we'll begin tomorrow afternoon.
>
> Best Regards, Eric Kramer

Hayley hugged me, beaming. "Mom, this is fantastic."

I did a happy dance around the room, laughing and clapping. "I can't believe I'm almost there. I've waited a lifetime to find her. Dreamed about it, visualized a reunion, prayed for her, and wished to see her. Now, with my permission, they'll call her tomorrow."

A frown crossed Hayley's brow. "Will it be better for them to call her instead of you? I know if I had to make the call, my stomach would tie up in knots."

"Yeah, me, too. I'd panic if I had to call her out of the blue. I'm relieved they'll be the ones to call her first, but this is what they do. I'm sure it isn't hard for them. I have butterflies. I so hope this is it."

"I guess after they contact her, she'll know you're looking. I wonder how she'll react."

"This is unfamiliar territory for me. I hope I can handle whatever happens."

I pushed print to save a copy of the letter. My mind filled with what ifs, but I needed to respond to Eric's request about my expectations. I wanted to state my intentions but word it in a way that I wouldn't alarm her.

My fingers tingled as I prepared the email.

> I'm excited to receive this! The information is coming to me much faster than I thought. As for my expectations, I'd like to establish a relationship, but not a mother-daughter one necessarily. I already have a loving adoptive mom. Meeting her would be great, and we could decide where to go from there. I don't want to scare her away. Receiving medical information would be helpful for me and my kids. My son, Nate, has Crohn's disease, so I'd be interested if anyone in her family had it. I approve of your making contact and hope you've found her. I'll be eager to hear from you again.

A quick response.

> I told you we're fast! We can typically complete a California case within one-to-three business days. We are not 100 percent certain of this woman yet; we'll verify her information. We'll call tomorrow between 4 – 5 p.m. central time. Afterward, we'll contact you. Thank you for placing your trust in us with this most delicate situation.
>
> Eric Kramer

I heard the door to the garage close. Dancing down the hall, I waved my arms and shouted, "Come and look at this email I got today, they think they've found her. Can you believe it's happened this fast? Look, read it all the way through. They're going to call her tomorrow."

Brent and Nate exchanged looks and chuckled.

I pulled them over to the computer and pointed to the message.

Brent sat down and read the email first. "Wow, they must have great resources to find someone in a couple of days."

Nate scanned the message over Brent's shoulder. "That's great, Mom."

After the kids went to bed, Brent and I sat on the edge of the bed going over various scenarios I might encounter.

"What do you think they'll say to her?"

Brent put his arm around my shoulder. "I don't know. He told you they're discreet. I'm sure they ask the right questions."

"True. I'm just afraid of getting my hopes up. I wonder if she will even be receptive to the call. I've visualized her having an open, caring personality. I have pictured her parents telling her to get on with her life after my birth. The closed adoption meant no contact, no point in trying to get information about me. I had always put a positive spin on the whole thing. I want her to be amazed I found her and willing to get to know me. I have a million questions."

"Yes, a happy ending. Are you worried it might not happen?"

I jumped off the bed, paced around the room. "What if she never wanted to be found? She never wants to meet me, talk to me, or have anything to do with me. Maybe it turned out to be the worst time in her life, and she felt traumatized by having me and giving me up. Finding her now could freak her out."

I picked up a tissue to stop the stream of tears. "Or maybe she agrees to meet me, but she's so bitter, angry, and disillusioned with how her life turned out, she ends up making us both miserable."

Brent stopped me from pacing and stood in front of me, taking both my hands. In a gentle voice, he said, "Either of those scenes could be true, except with the second one, you'd at least be able to meet her and see what she looks like."

I closed my eyes and tipped my head back. "Yeah, it would be better than nothing, I guess, but now I want it all. The happy ending, great relationship, and healing."

He squeezed my hands and pulled me into a hug. Smiling at him, I sighed.

Mulling over the events from the day, I pulled out my journal.

March 1

What a day it turned out to be! They hope to make contact tomorrow with a woman who might be my birth mother. Wow. Scary, happy, nervous. How to contain all my feelings. Talking with Brent gave me perspective. This could be wonderful or horrible. I'm only in control of my feelings, not the outcome. I pray for her often, realizing this isn't only about me. Her feelings play a big part in all this, too, whether good, bad, or indifferent. At least I can rest in the fact God already knows how she feels about my birth and adoption. He's watching over her the same way He's watched over me. I'd never want to do anything to jeopardize her current situation. Maybe she has a husband and family she's never told about me. Yikes, talk about awkward. I'm hoping for a relationship we'll both be comfortable with. I pray meeting me will heal any hurt she's suffered. I also want to close the gap caused by not knowing my roots. I have a broken circle. Missing pieces, incomplete info, not feeling whole.

Thinking about her makes me wonder about my birth father. If her last name had been Long, could his have been Donovan? Did she give me his last name? I haven't given him a lot of consideration. It's always been about finding the woman who carried me for nine months, gave me up, and signed the papers. I don't even know if she told him about her pregnancy. I want to ask her about him, too.

As I pray tonight, I ask for the possibility of a reunion. Please have her mind and heart, as well as mine, prepared for the events about to unfold. God's will be done in both our lives and the courage to accept whatever path He's chosen for us.

CHAPTER FIVE

"Hurry you two, I've got to get home. Fact Finders is calling today." The wholesale store was crowded. Hundreds of people pushing giant shopping carts looking for bargains. Brent and Nate loved to look around and go down every aisle. Standing in the long line at the checkout didn't calm my nerves.

I was so anxious I was bouncing on my toes. I had a million questions running through my mind. Did she answer the phone? Would I get information on her? Is this her?

At exactly five p.m., the phone rang. I almost tripped over Nate rushing to the kitchen to get the phone.

"May I speak to Patrish? This is Eric at Fact Finders."

My hands trembled. "Hi, Eric, this is Patrish. How's everything going?" I cleared my voice to get rid of the squeak.

"We made contact today with the woman believed to have been your birth mother, however, she denied any knowledge of your birth details. I'm sorry for the false alarm, but she appeared to be the right one."

I looked down and closed my eyes, but my voice still faltered. I looked over at Brent and shook my head. "Oh, I'm disappointed. I hoped we'd find her right away. What happens next?"

"We still have two strong matches meeting our search criteria. We're in the process of trying to locate them. We'll make phone contact to verify our data. I know you'd hoped this would be it, but don't give up. We'll keep going until we find her."

"Thank you, Eric." I couldn't hide the disappointment in my voice. "Please thank everyone who is working on this for me. I'll be waiting to hear what happens with the other two possibilities."

"We'll contact you with any new developments. It'll most likely take a day or two."

Hanging up, I growled. "This is so typical."

"Hey, Mom, I hate to ask how it went," Nate commented as he walked into the kitchen.

"You heard my end of the conversation. They haven't found her yet. They boast of having a 97 percent success rate. I hope I don't fall into the 3 percent failure category. The good thing is they still have two other women to check out. He told me not to give up, and they'll keep going until they find her."

Nate gave me a small smile. "At least it's something to hope for."

Brent had been standing beside me in the kitchen and heard what I told Nate.

He reached out and touched my shoulder. "I'm glad you feel hopeful. I know this is hard."

"I knew it could happen." I plopped down on the kitchen stool. "This entire process is making me jumpy. Look at my hands shaking, and it's only been a couple of days. I'm going to look on the computer. Maybe they have meetings where people talk about their experiences."

I went to the computer and pondered my next move. My hands hesitated over the keyboard. Back to basics. I typed in *Adoptee Support Groups in San Diego*. I found a local group, Adoptee Awareness Support. They included anyone in the triad of birth mothers, adoptees, and adoptive parents; they met once a month. I clapped my hands. One step closer.

I rubbed the back of my neck. What's next?

Call Mom.

We chatted about my brother Josh, Brent's job, and my sister Lindsay's latest adventure. As if reading my mind, Mom set up the conversation with a simple "Is there anything else going on?"

I plunged in. "Yes, as a matter of fact, there is. On Monday, I contacted a company to look for my birth mother."

Without the slightest hesitation, she said, "Good. Where did you find the company?"

I told her how I'd found Fact Finders and what I'd learned so far.

"I've always known how much this means to you. Remember, I'll help you in any way I can. I don't know what more I could do but keep me in the loop. I want to know how everything goes."

I sighed. "The hardest part is waiting to hear from them. I don't want it to be long and drawn out."

"When Blake searched for his birth parents in the eighties, he had to do everything manually. He found a book with agencies to contact and sent out dozens of inquiry letters. This sounds a lot easier."

"I remember him doing that. My determined brother wouldn't give up, and he found his birth father."

"I know I couldn't believe it. I'll never forget his emotions. He and I drove to the address we found for his birth father," said Mom. "Blake couldn't sit still in the car and didn't talk. He wanted to meet his dad by himself. I went along for moral support. His birth father's wife invited him into the house."

"I can imagine how nervous you both were. How long did you have to wait in the car?"

"He stayed inside for about forty-five minutes. It felt like forever, but then they strolled out to the car together. It struck me how Blake had the same stride as his dad, and they had a similar build. He introduced himself, and we left. As we drove off, I couldn't wait to hear how it went."

"I don't remember the whole story. What did they say to each other?"

"His dad hadn't heard from Blake's mom in years. Blake kept saying over and over how amazing it was to have found him. He laughed and smiled all the way home. I beamed, too. They promised to keep in touch, and I think he did see him a few times."

"Then he came to Blake's funeral." Tears welled up in my eyes.

"We were all so upset I don't think any of us spoke to him."

I heard Mom blow into a tissue. "I didn't even know he was there, Mom."

"What a sad way for their relationship to end." Mom cleared her throat. "Well, I hope you hear from them soon, and it turns out the way you want it to."

I felt a headache coming on. "Thanks, Mom. I appreciate how you've always been supportive. I'll let you know when I hear from them."

That evening, I turned to my journal.

March 2

I'm having a hard time being patient with this waiting game. It's only been three days but feels longer. All these mixed emotions. What will she think when they call her? Back in 1955, information couldn't be found like today. They told her the adoption was closed. No one would know or come looking for her. What had been her story? How did her life unfold? Looking back in time, being pregnant was socially unacceptable. Unwed mothers often brought shame to the family. According to the info I received, her mom supported her decision for adoption. I wonder if she went through her days trying to hide the pregnancy. She contacted the adoption agency and made all the plans. Then she went home without me. What happened next? Did she find a job, move away from her memories and parents? Did she marry, but never tell him about what she went through? Never speaking of it to anyone again, including her parents? Her secret was safe. Along came the computer age. There is never a convenient time to blurt out, "Oh, by the way, at the age of twenty-six, I got pregnant and gave my daughter up for adoption."

What's hidden remains hidden. It sounds exhausting. Keeping a secret must be a huge, stressful burden.

I need to remain optimistic and wait for the search to be narrowed down. Where to next?

My Bible verse for today seems appropriate. Proverbs 3: 5-6... "Trust in the Lord with all your heart and lean not on your own understanding; in all your ways submit to Him and He will make your paths straight."

CHAPTER SIX

arch 2, I waited all day to hear what Fact Finders had discovered. I checked my emails every hour. Nothing. So, time to contact them.

> Hi, Eric. Is there anything new with my search?

The response came later that day.

> We're working hard on your data; we have about twenty-five possible women we need to investigate further. These women all share the same common last name of Long and are the appropriate age. It will take a little time to pursue all the information we need to sort out. We hope to have your results within a few more business days, but we can't promise you it will happen fast. We understand you're feeling anxious, so please bear with us, and we'll provide another update in a few days. Have a great weekend.
>
> Best Regards, Eric

A warmth and peace settled into hope after the agonizing days of waiting. Maybe researching twenty-five women would tip the odds in my favor. The next few days came and went. Hours were sluggish. I jumped at every ding of the computer.

"Mom, you already asked us what we wanted for dinner. Why did you ask again?" Hayley narrowed her eyes and smirked.

"Sorry, I'm distracted. Not knowing what Fact Finders has found out is driving me crazy. I've gone into the bedroom three times but forgot what I was looking for." I looked directly at my daughter. "How do you feel about me trying to find my birth mother? It'd mean finding another grandmother, a biological grandmother."

"Seems kind of weird to me since we already have Grandma. I don't think about her being your adoptive mom. She's our grandma with the fun swimming pool, big house, and great laugh."

I turned to Nate. "How about you?"

"I know it's a big deal to you, but I don't think of anyone else as your mom. Grandma's the one we see all the time. When you and Dad go out of town, we go to her house. When all the cousins come to San Diego, we all go to see her. This other person will be a stranger to us. Maybe she won't accept us as her grandchildren."

"Good point. We would all have some adjusting to do if she came into our lives. She's a stranger to me, too. If they do find her, she would have to agree to meet me. At the rate this is going, we may have a long time to think about it."

On March 11, the email came from Fact Finders.

> Your search is proving to be difficult; many of the women on our list of possibilities are turning out to be deceased. I have one research assistant assigned to your case and forwarded your info to another to have her access it as well. I'm hoping we can still complete this process for you. I will send you an update soon.
>
> Best Regards, Eric.

"You have *got* to be kidding me," I shouted through clenched teeth to the empty game room. My voice echoed off the high ceiling in the room. I stood and threw my hands up.

Am I the only one whose birth mother is untraceable?

Brent came home to find me slumped over the computer, my head down and my eyes closed.

I heard him drop his briefcase on the table, then he came into the room. "You're frowning. Did anything happen to the kids, or did you get bad news?"

Blurry eyed, I answered, "Take a look at this message I received today. Now I have two more things to worry about. They may not be able to complete this at all, or she could already be dead." I burst into tears. "I don't want her to be dead. It would mean she died too young. I wouldn't get to know her or ask her questions. Why can't they find her? I have a pounding headache and a heartache to match."

Brent kneeled by my chair. "Don't give up yet. They didn't say they were going to stop looking. They're trying to figure out what new angles they can work."

Wiping tears off my cheek, I turned to him. "I know it's not time to panic yet. Fact Finders told me if they find out she's no longer alive, they will still give me all her information. Her full name, last address, and if she'd married or had other children. If that happens, I want to know when and how she died." I groaned. "This can't end yet, not this way."

Brent leaned in and kissed me. "God will work this out. You'll see. He never wants us to worry or doubt His miracles. What's meant to be will be. I want you to have your dreams come true. Meet her, talk with her, get closure. I'm here for you at every turn."

I wrapped my arms around his neck. "Thank you. I know I can count on both you and God. I appreciate your patience with me."

The next week I stayed away from the computer. Writing in my journal, I put down all the events of the last few weeks, including the emails I'd received and how disillusioned I felt.

Nate traipsed into the kitchen. "Hey, Mom, are you going to do the laundry today? I'm running out of T-shirts."

"Oh, yeah, sorry." I shook my head. "I'll start a load right now."

Hayley came through the front door. "You look preoccupied, Mom."

"I'm thinking about Fact Finders. I don't know why I'm always the one to contact them. I haven't had an update in a while. Maybe no news is good news."

After starting the laundry, I sent them an email. I waited, then received:

> I heard from the assistant assigned to your case. She says she's eliminated all possibilities except five. She's currently checking them out. I'll email you again as soon as I have more news for you. I hope to be contacting you next week.

> **Thank you, sounds great. I'll keep my fingers crossed and pray she's one of the five women. I look forward to hearing from you.**

I pressed my hands to my temples, reading their next reply.

> In addition, we'll need to hope she's still alive, as our records indicate not all five of the women are.

Hayley watched my response. "Uh-oh, you look distressed. What did they say?"

I read her the email, then I said, "Now I'm back to wondering if she's alive and waiting for their next email."

"You'll get through this, Mom."

"Thanks for the encouragement. I'm going to call Grandma and give her an update."

After Mom's cheery hello, she asked, "What's going on with the search?"

"That's why I'm calling. They seem to be stalled. They're narrowing it down, but I need to think about the fact she might not be alive."

"I can hear it in your voice. You're feeling defeated. They're not giving up, are they?"

"No, Fact Finders wants to complete the search. Of course, it could end with her being deceased. I shouldn't be upset. It's only been a month, but my patience is being tested."

"Hang in there. Good things come to those who wait."

"Thanks, Mom. I'm lucky to have you."

I wandered to the office. I decided it was time for another journal entry.

March 25

I keep thinking about these women they'll contact. Is this the last group of women she could be in? What do I do if they can't find her, and I end up right back where I was twenty-six days ago? How do they figure out who she is if she's not alive? They can't verify anything. I know I repeat myself when I say the waiting is doing me in. A week isn't too long to wait. I'd feel better if I could sleep or these questions would stop bouncing around in my head. Is it easy for someone to hide their identity? If she doesn't want to be found, she's doing a good job of hiding. They've told me two times this has been difficult. Every time I hear it, I can't help but wonder if my birth mother was the first person they spoke to way back in the beginning. She could have denied whatever they asked her and remained anonymous. Not a good sign. This is the reason I was hesitant to look for her. It took me a long time to get up my nerve. Now I wonder what in the world I've gotten myself into. I hope it doesn't take them more than a week to get back to me.

My daily routine of reading the Bible helps. It reminds me to keep my focus on God. I've been self-absorbed.

I need to rely on what I know is true. God's watching over me and working all things out for the good of all who believe in Him. Matthew 6:34 reminds me, "Therefore, do not worry about tomorrow, for tomorrow will worry about itself. Each day has enough trouble of its own." Amen and Amen!

CHAPTER SEVEN

One week later, I heard the ping on the computer. A new message. I let out a heavy sigh and hit the key to open the email. "Not again," I growled, folding my arms across my chest.

> Nothing new to report currently. My assistant, Rita, is sorting things out in your case. I'll send you an email as soon as something changes. Please be patient and bear with us as your case is very time consuming.

There were those annoying words again. A sudden tiredness overtook me. Ping, another email.

> Rita discovered one woman she'd been focused on is deceased. We'll have to wait for a copy of the death certificate to see if it matches the info we have.

Ugh. I slumped in my chair. I knew I needed to shake it off. I took a calming breath, picked up the phone, and called my sister-in-law, Jackie. I knew she would cheer me up.

We caught up on everyone's activities before I jumped into the reason for the call.

"Remember when I started collecting info about my birth mother because someday, I wanted to find her? That day is here." I described the details and how it had progressed.

"I'm so glad you decided to do it," she said in her warm, caring voice. "Right now, you're emotional, but it will be worth it. Fear held you back for such a long time. Being afraid is okay, the unknown is always scary. Look at all you've accomplished by working through it. Have you been praying about it?"

"You bet. I pray every day for God's will to be done." My voice became stronger, and I said with conviction, "I don't know her circumstances. Maybe seeing me would be harmful emotionally, or maybe she'd be healed from a lifetime of hurting. I don't know, but God is in control. Please, keep me in your prayers."

"You know I will. I'll put a prayer request in at church, too, so the entire staff will be praying for you to stay strong. I have your back. We'll get through this together."

"Thanks, Jackie. I can always count on you."

I hung up and stretched my limbs. Time to move on to other things. No more negative.

Journal writing time.

April 1

I need to consider the facts; she might not be alive or she's hiding from Fact Finders. The agency listed her age as twenty-six when she had me, making her birth year 1929. So, she's seventy-six now. Doesn't seem old to me; I don't know if she had any health issues. I'd love to find out ways we're alike. Do you get migraine headaches? Does anyone in your family have Crohn's disease? Are you allergic to bee stings? Do you love to laugh? Or read? Will we feel an instant connection when we meet? Who is my birth father?

Maybe this week will bring good news.

CHAPTER EIGHT

Tuesday rolled into Wednesday then Thursday. I checked and rechecked the emails. Nothing. On April 7, we had spaghetti night.

"Nate, will you please bring the French bread? Hayley, you can help me carry the salads. Dad should be home any minute."

Nate grabbed the bread wrapped in foil. "There's the garage door."

Brent rubbed his belly when he walked into the kitchen. "It smells good in here. I love spaghetti."

"We're eating an early dinner tonight, so I'm glad you're home now."

We filled our plates, sat together, said grace, then dug in.

"What's new at work, Brent?" I asked.

He started to answer when the phone ringing interrupted us. I jumped up to grab it.

Eric was on the line.

"I came into my office and found a note from Rita. She's 99 percent positive we've found your birth mother."

"Who is it?" Brent asked.

I waved my hand to stop him from speaking. "This is incredible news," I squealed, dancing around the room. "What happens next?"

I looked over at my family's blank stares. I held up one finger to let them know I'd fill them in after the call.

"We'll need to verify it's her. Do you want to make the first contact, or do you want us to call?"

"Making the first call is too scary for me," I mumbled. "I wouldn't know what to say. I'd rather you contact her."

"Would you like to think about it and call me back?"

"No, I'm positive. When will you call?"

Eric's voice was strong and confident. "Rita will call her tonight. If this is indeed your birth mother, we'll be able to give you all the information we've collected. I need to remind you, if this doesn't go well, and she rejects you, we will still require payment. We conduct about five searches a week and have an average of one rejection a month."

The kids continued eating. Brent's eyes were focused on me.

I asked Eric, "I've known all along it could be possible. I understand the payment is due. When would I get the information?"

Eric said, "After we get confirmation, we'll call you and get your credit card number. Her name will be released to you, and I'll email you a detailed report in a couple of days. Please tell me again what kind of relationship you'd like to have with her. Birth mothers often need reassurance after being contacted."

"I don't want to scare her off. I'd like to be able to meet and see where our relationship goes from there." I gave Brent a thumbs up.

"Okay, Rita will convey your feelings. I'll call you back in a couple of hours."

I put down the phone and shouted, "Yes!"

"Now we're all curious," said Brent. "Obviously that was Eric. What did he say?"

Skipping around the table, I grabbed Brent's arm. "He stated they really believe they found her. Eric felt sure about it. You heard my end of the conversation. Rita's calling her right now. This is where reality hits. I may be able to meet her soon, or I might get a rude awakening. But right now, I feel like dancing for joy."

Brent laughed. "It's good to see you happy and optimistic, but your spaghetti is getting cold."

"I don't know if I can eat. Too many thoughts and a jumpy stomach. He told me he'd call back tonight."

Hayley and Nate looked at each other, smiling.

"We're glad to see you're happy, Mom," said Hayley. "The last few days were rough."

"Thanks. I know my mood affects you guys, too. We don't know where this is leading yet."

Staring at the phone didn't make it ring any sooner, but at eight o'clock, the call finally came.

I could tell by the tone of Eric's voice this wasn't exciting news. "Rita hasn't been able to reach anyone yet. It's getting late here in Michigan. We'll try again first thing in the morning. I can give you the facts we've gathered. If this is your birth mother, we found a lot of information on her and her parents. We know this person is married and has a daughter. I'll give you all the facts after we speak with her. I'll call you Thursday after two in the afternoon your time."

Here we go again. Just like a long car ride with the question, *Are we there yet?*

Absentminded, I meandered into the bedroom, forgot why I went in there, then returned to the kitchen to finish washing the dishes. The kids finished homework in their rooms, and Brent made phone calls. I sat on the couch and picked up the book I'd been reading. Ten minutes later, I stood. I'd read the same paragraph over and over but couldn't remember what it said.

"This is ridiculous," I muttered under my breath.

Brent finished his calls, and we got ready for bed. I pulled the covers up to my chin. My mind kept spinning scenarios. Was this an adventure or a cliff? Restless, I tossed and turned. I kept coming back to the phrase, let go and let God.

Thursday's pace felt like slugging through mud. I looked at the clock every half an hour wishing two o'clock would hurry up. At two ten, I jumped when the phone rang. It was Eric.

"Every time we call, the answering machine picks up. We aren't giving up. We will speak to her. Rita will call today and tomorrow," said Eric.

"Does she live in California?" I asked, letting out the breath I'd been holding.

"Yes," he answered. "We hope that will make connecting with her easier for you. I'll contact you as soon as we speak with her. Most likely it will be tomorrow."

Tomorrow. Good grief. I've come this far, I'm not turning back. The kids and Brent were gone, and the empty house held an eerie silence. I could hear the dogs barking down the street and smell the banana bread I'd warmed up for breakfast.

It was time to pick the kids up from school. My daily routine continued.

Friday, April 8, I puttered around the house after getting the kids off to school. Brent waited with me.

The phone rang announcing Eric's call. Brent and I looked at each other.

Eric said, "I'm sorry to tell you the phone call didn't go well. The woman we called is the person we were looking for. Before I give you any information, we need to process the payment."

I put my hand over my heart and let out a whimper. Brent's gaze stayed focused on me. I felt tears in my eyes as I looked at him and shook my head. I robotically gave Eric my card information. I could barely see the imprinted numbers.

Eric sounded sympathetic. "Your birth mother's name is Nora Bower. She and her husband Ross live in Palm Desert. Her maiden name's Long. She was born July 1, 1929. Rita commented that when they spoke, she wasn't receptive. Nora seemed agitated and unwilling to cooperate. She didn't deny any of the facts Rita presented but kept saying 'I can't help you.' Rita had a final question for her. 'May I ask you one more question? Haven't you ever wondered about the daughter you gave birth to?' Nora's answer had been brisk. 'I'm not going to tell you anything. I didn't ask you to do this.' She hung up on Rita. I'm sorry it turned out this way, Patrish. I do have more family history if you're ready to hear it."

I tried not to cry, but my voice cracked. "I want to hear whatever you found."

Eric continued. "Her mother's name was Victoria Long. Born November 1, 1910. She died in 1995. Victoria's husband's name turned out to be Gene. Date of birth, November 5, 1906, and death in 1995. Gene died from acute heart disease, and Victoria died from pneumonia. Nora and Ross have been married since June 1956. They have one daughter, Katie. Her birthday is April 11, 1957. We believe Katie has been married twice and has a twenty-two-year-old daughter Janine."

My mind raced. Brent's pained expression conveyed love.

"This is a lot of information. Wow, I have a sister close to my age. My grandfather's birthday is the same day as mine. This is mind boggling." Numbness set in. It became difficult to jot down notes. Everything was coming so fast.

"Yes, I know all this is a lot to take in. You shouldn't take what she said personally. Nora doesn't know you. She must have been upset to get a phone call asking personal questions. Most of the time, a reaction like this means they haven't told anyone about what happened in the past."

I winced. "It *feels* very personal. Are you positive she's my birth mother? What do you use for verification?"

"We got a copy of the driver's license. The description is the same as the one in your non-identifying info sheet. All these facts will be included in an email containing the receipt. I do want to tell you Nora had been the first woman we contacted in the search. She told us she wasn't who we were looking for. We feel we can't contact her any further. She won't be receptive to hearing from us a third time. You'll get her address and phone number. You can decide how you want to handle getting in touch with her. Fact Finders would still like to help you locate a biological family member. Would you be open to contacting Katie?"

My ears started ringing, and I couldn't catch my breath. Brent rushed over to me and put his arm across my shoulders. Blinking rapidly, I looked into his eyes. I needed to stay calm and finish this conversation.

"What process do you use to find her? Do you have her address and phone number?"

"Rita found an address in a small town outside L.A., but no phone number. There is a business fax number we can use to ask her to call us. Do we have your permission to make contact today?"

"I'm having trouble processing all the info you gave me. I guess Katie would be a good avenue to pursue. It'd be nice to meet someone in my family."

"Rita will fax her today. If this doesn't work, we will send a letter. You'll get to see a copy before we send it."

"I hope she calls you back. Let me know how it goes," my voice quivered.

I put the receiver down. A cold, blankness rushed over me. My worst nightmare had become reality. My birth mother rejected me again.

Brent asked, "Are you going to be all right? I should get to the office, but I can stay longer if you need me to."

"No, you can go. I'm still trying to wrap my mind around all this. We'll talk tonight when I'm more coherent."

He kissed me goodbye.

I spent the whole day staring at my notes. I read and reread all the facts Eric had told me about my first family. Nora had been difficult to talk to. She had hung up on Rita. No remorse expressed, no answer as to whether she had ever thought about me again. I rubbed my hands over my cheeks. I made a timeline of Nora's life, from my conception to Katie's birth.

I couldn't hold back the tears any longer. They streamed down my face for the little baby girl whisked away from her birth mother. A baby left in the hospital. Alone. A knot formed in my chest for the rejection I felt when I was old enough to understand she didn't want me. I sobbed, burying my face in my hands. I was crushed that she didn't want to meet me. Her life went along as if I'd never been born.

I slammed my fist on the table.

I confronted my husband when he came through the garage door into the house. "You're not going to believe this, Brent." I waved a paper in front of him.

"I've made a timeline out of the facts I got from Eric. Katie and I are only seventeen months apart. I was only eight months old when her mom got pregnant with her. My adoption had just been finalized. She and Ross were newly married. It only took her seventeen months to have another child."

Brent put his arms around me. "I know it feels like a raw wound right now. Maybe giving you up turned out to be the hardest thing Nora had done, causing her to not be able to meet you. We don't know the circumstances around the decision."

I threw my hands up. "That's what gets me. I may never know how she felt. I can't believe she hung up on Rita. She didn't even consider my feelings. I held out for the warm, fuzzy reunion. The kind you see on TV where everyone's hugging and crying. Now, I'm the only one crying, and not from joy."

Brent sighed. "I heard you asking about contacting Katie. That would be one way to find out about Nora."

My shoulders drooped. "Yeah, it's better than nothing, I guess. But Nora has always been the one I wanted to meet."

I headed to the bedroom to write in my journal. Maybe writing would help me make sense of everything I'd learned. The words came out in jerky motions. My tears continued, and I reached for yet another tissue.

Would I ever understand this path? I dislike the phrase *why me,* but it kept replaying in my head. I recalled David Jeremiah telling his readers that God is still God. And He's weaving the good and the bad together to create a masterpiece. I looked upward at the ceiling. *Sorry, God, right now I don't feel like a masterpiece, only a mess.*

CHAPTER NINE

I woke up with red, swollen eyes. Great, now I even look like a mess. Saturdays were less hectic. No rushing off to school or early food prep. I shuffled into the kitchen to get a glass of water. The kids and Brent were finishing their breakfast.

"Hi guys," I croaked.

Brent smiled. "What do you have going on this morning?"

"Getting ready to look at my emails." My smile didn't reach my eyes. "I wonder what today will bring."

"Nate and I both need rides. I'm going over to Rachael's this afternoon, and Nate is going to John's." She looked at her brother and Nate nodded.

"I can take you later. I'm mowing the lawn this morning," said Brent.

Just around the corner from the bar, I turned on the computer. There was an email from Eric. I read it out loud.

> We haven't heard from Katie. I would like to wait another
> day before formulating a letter to send to her.

I turned to Brent. "I love the fact I have a half sister in this world. I admit I'm nervous about Fact Finders contacting her. It'll be a shock to find out about me. It could put a strain between her and Nora. All this time, Katie was an only daughter. Now, without warning, there's a big sister in the picture. She might feel Nora's been lying to her all this time. What a big, ugly sore this is turning out to be."

"The other side of the picture could be Nora feeling relieved everything's out in the open. Carrying a secret can be a huge burden. Although, I do have to say her initial reaction doesn't seem to be one of relief. I feel bad for you, Patrish."

"I hope Katie's more curious about me than Nora is. It would be great to get to know her. Maybe I could see pictures of Nora and hear about Katie's childhood. Maybe someday Nora would give in and meet me. You know what's crazy? Katie's birthday is in two days, April 11. Happy surprise birthday, you have a big sister!"

"That will be a surprise. Let's hope it's a welcome one."

Later that evening, I heard the computer ping with a new email. I took a loud, crunchy bite from my apple and opened the message from Eric.

> We researched the information concerning Katie Bower's residence. It appears she no longer lives there. We could send her a letter and hope it gets forwarded. However, we're concerned she may be living at her mom's. We'd like to take another day to think about how to approach this.

"On and on it goes," I muttered between bites. "Lord, give me patience."

On Monday, I checked the emails every fifteen minutes for messages. One came in at noon.

> I think we may have made a little progress today. Rita and I spent the last few hours on your case. We learned Katie Bower was married to Lou Hale. They have a daughter named Janine. We called the number we found for her. Someone at their residence took our number to have Janine call us back tomorrow. We're guessing it may have been a roommate. We'll wait to see if she contacts

us. If we don't hear from her, we'll call again tomorrow evening. I'll keep you posted.

I twisted in my chair. Sitting here rereading the email wasn't getting me anywhere. I decided to put my energy to good use. Our backyard has a steep hill covered in bushes, plants, and weeds. We never had to plant anything on the hill. Nature took care of the growth. The bushes needed trimming, and the weeds had to be removed. I put on my gardening gloves, grabbed the clippers, and went to work. I yanked the weeds out as if they were all my bad thoughts. Muttering under my breath, I complained about the unfairness of the situation. The pile of weeds grew as I plucked with vengeance. How dare they treat me as if I don't exist. I'm a person, too. Nora knows who I am, whether she wants Katie to know or not. Pull, pluck, tear, snip. I looked around with a satisfied nod.

Brent came home early that evening. He looked out the window at my work. "Wow, you've been busy. What made you take on the backyard?"

Pulling up the email from Fact Finders, I announced, "Read this. It's starting to get complicated. Now Katie and her daughter Janine will know about Nora's past. She kept it quiet for fifty years. One phone call and I've forced the truth on everyone. I don't think they're going to be happy with me."

He read it and looked over at me. "It won't be easy for Nora to explain this away. She'll have to tell them something about what happened. You're right,"—he nodded—"Nora and Katie will probably be upset. Janine is younger. This might not bother her as much."

"Now you see why I took it out on the hill. At least I did something constructive. I think the yard looks great." I felt good about my work, and I grinned at Brent. "The kids asked for sloppy joes tonight. Dinner will be ready in half an hour. They're in their rooms doing homework."

"Okay, I'll go say hi to them. Great job on the hill."

It took another day for Eric to get back to me.

We received a phone call from Janine. She heard our
message and promised to pass Rita's phone number on
to her mom. We hope to hear from Katie soon.

I wrinkled my nose. Would this be good news or bad? Another
slow process or could it be fast? I thought about every detail of this
search. Twists and turns, unexpected feelings. I let out a slow breath.
I'm on this ride no matter what I find.

It took two more days to get another email from Eric.

We haven't heard from Katie yet. We may have to think
about another way to make contact. How do you feel
about sending the letter I told you about? It would go to
Katie through Janine. We still don't have an address for
Katie, only Janine.

I frowned through another exchange:

How will you place Katie's letter in the envelope
addressed to Janine? Will it be in another envelope with
Katie's name on the outside? Or will Janine be able to
read it, too?

We want to keep it as private as possible. We'll put the
letter inside another envelope and place Katie's name on
it. I'll spend the rest of today drafting the letter and email
it to you for approval.

I had mixed feelings about the letter. Oh boy, here we go. How
will they word all the information to let Katie know about me?

A few hours later, I received my answer, it made me smile. The
letter read:

Dear Katie,

Since I've been unable to speak with you on the phone, I decided to send you this information regarding a possible relative who is trying to find birth family members.

Patrish was born 11-5-55 in San Diego, California, and given up for adoption at birth. She has obtained background information from a private adoption agency. This is a summary of the information about her birth mother and parents.

Birth mother maiden name: Long

State of residence: California

Age at birth of child: 26 years old, born 1929 in California.

Birthday: July 1

Physical description: blonde hair, blue eyes, 5'6"

Slender features, no siblings

Her father: age 49, 5'10" tall, dark hair and eyes

Her mother: age 45, 5'5" tall, dark hair, green eyes

Our research revealed the following names of the family members:

Mother's maiden name: Winston

Her parents: Gene Long, born 11-5-1906

Victoria Long, born 11-1-1910

After reading this, please let us know if you believe you could be a half sister to Patrish. Please feel free to either call me at the number above or contact me by email. We have much more information we're anxious to share with you and would prefer to communicate directly. We

hope you understand and accept Patrish's curiosity in
the positive spirit she intended.

The letter conveyed straightforward, undisputable facts. No malice directed at anyone, only an interest in finding family members. I typed my email approval for sending the letter. Janine lived in Georgia, so I knew I needed to be patient while waiting for a response. I straightened my back. Now would be the perfect time to go to an Adoptee Awareness meeting. Looking up the site, I saw the next meeting would be held on April 14.

CHAPTER TEN

My stomach growled as I drove to the meeting in La Mesa. I only picked at my food during dinner, unable to enjoy the chicken I'd prepared. I kept looking at the clock and shifting in my seat the entire meal. I had no idea what to expect at the meeting.

Strolling through the doors of the recreation center, I stopped and looked around. There was a small kitchen area straight ahead, and on the left, a room with chairs arranged in a circle and a few tables in the back. In the entryway, a man was placing brochures on a small table. Wearing a T-shirt and jeans, he appeared to be in his thirties. Two people sitting in the circle of chairs were chatting.

I ran my sweaty palms down my pant legs and approached the man at the table to introduce myself.

"Hi, I'm Patrish. Is this the Adoptee Awareness group?"

"Hi, and yes, you're in the right place. I'm Paul."

"This is my first time," I replied, wringing my hands.

"Welcome, we're glad you came. Why don't you go ahead and sign in on this sheet and find a seat. We'll begin at seven."

I signed my name and found a seat. A petite Asian woman with long dark hair, sat to my left in an overstuffed chair by the lamp.

Note to self—get here early next time to get one of those chairs.

Across from me was another woman who looked to be close to my age.

The three of us exchanged hellos, as two more men and two women came through the doors. They greeted each other and seemed to know one another well.

Paul facilitated the meeting. He asked everyone to find a seat, so we could get started.

"Let's go around the room and introduce yourselves. Tell us where you fit in the adoption triad, and how your reunion is going, if you're in one." He paused as if letting that all sink in. "I'll go first. My name is Paul, I'm an adopted person, and I've been in reunion with my birth mom for ten years."

Wow, he's traveled down roads I haven't even begun to see.

Paul looked to his right. A pretty redhead introduced herself. "I'm Carla, an adoptee, and I've been in reunion for one month."

Next the petite woman spoke. "I'm Gina, an adoptee. I'm not in reunion, but I'm looking for my birth parents in Korea."

Now it was my turn. I'd never been in a group of people who were all adopted and willing to speak openly about it. I took a deep breath.

"I'm Patrish, an adoptee. I went through the process, but my birth mother rejected me." Uninvited tears blurred my vision.

Paul looked at me. "After we have everyone introduce themselves, we'll go around the circle, get more details from each of you. We're all anxious to hear your story, Patrish."

I nodded, clasped my hands between my knees, and looked at the others in the group. I received small smiles of acceptance and understanding nods.

The man sitting next to me smiled and spoke next. "I'm Brad, an adoptee, and both my parents died before I found them. I'm in reunion with my brother and sister."

"I'm Jolene, an adoptee. I'm not in reunion because my birth mother told me she had nothing to say to me." She looked right at me when she spoke. Her brown eyes softened, connecting with mine.

The woman to Jolene's right leaned forward in her seat. Her gray curls framing her face. "My name is Brita, I'm a birth mother. I'm in a semi reunion with my thirty-six-year-old son. It isn't going as well as I'd hoped, but at least we're communicating through emails."

A birth mother? This should be interesting. I can't wait to hear what she has to say.

The last person in the group wore shorts and a T-shirt. Leaning back in his chair, he said, "My name is Roberto, I'm an adoptee. I've been in reunion with my birth mother for about fifteen years and my birth father for three years."

Paul turned to Carla. "Tell us how it's going Carla. You're still in the early stages of reunion. How do you feel about your relationship with your birth mother?"

She laughed, spreading her arms out. "I'm amazed to find all these people out there who are related to me. My birth mom invited me to a get-together at her house. All her sisters were there, along with nieces, nephews, and my two half sisters. Growing up, I only had one brother, one uncle, and three aunts."

"You're still in the honeymoon stage," Paul said to her and looked at me to explain. "The honeymoon stage refers to the early stages of reunion. It feels wonderful, you get along with your birth parent, and everything is rosy. It usually doesn't last."

"I know it won't last." Carla sighed. "Even now, I can feel her being evasive. There are facts about my birth she has no intention of telling me. I could tell that just by the looks she gave her sister when we were all together. I asked her questions and panic filled her eyes. She crossed her arms and tried to cover up by changing the subject. There are things I want to know. I don't think I'll ever hear the whole story. She seems so secretive."

Paul leaned forward and placed his elbows on his knees. "What do you want her to tell you?"

Carla ran her hand through her hair. "I want the details of my story. How my birth parents met, my birth father's name, where he lives, if their relationship had been serious. You know, the works."

I watched wide eyed at the rest of the group's reactions to Carla. Gina nodded, Brad looked down at his feet, Jolene kept a steady gaze on Carla.

"It's hard when you don't know your complete story," Jolene added. "I've had to piece mine together. I don't know if I'll ever find out more."

Carla scooted to the edge of her chair. "I'm glad I found her. I want to keep this relationship going. I like to be upfront and ask direct questions, but she doesn't seem to want to answer them."

"Your relationship will go through a series of changes as you get to know each other," Roberto chimed in. "Sooner or later, we all have to deal with the secrets attached to adoption."

"Ah, yes, all the big secrets." Paul shook his head. "How we love being someone's *big* secret. We also sympathize with birth mothers like you, Brita. Eventually, we all pay a pretty hefty price for all the cover up."

Brita frowned. "We never get over the pain of relinquishment. They told me not to look for my son. It made me happy when he looked for me. The big secret is all a part of the shame everyone heaps on you. Your parents wonder how you could have embarrassed them. Other people look at you like you're a bad person."

"The strange part is they never emphasize trying to keep the mother and baby together. In our cases, adoptive parents were the only ones who seemed fit. Things are different now," added Carla.

Brita's eyes lit up, and her voice was strong with conviction. "You're right. No one came forward and even suggested my baby should stay with me. My family seemed adamant adoptive parents would do a better job. At twenty-two, I would've made it work somehow."

Paul nodded. "Gina, how are the plans going for your second trip to Korea? You leave in about a month, right?"

Gina settled back into the big, comfortable chair. "Yeah, I don't have much time to get everything ready. My Korean lessons are progressing. I hope I'll be able to communicate with the woman at the orphanage this time. I'm glad I won't need a translator because I want her to feel my emotions, but I'm still counting on a long shot."

Brad turned to Gina. "I admire how much work you're going through to reach your goal. No matter how much the rest of us had to go through, your search is the hardest. You have to travel to another country, learn a new language, and deal with all the red tape an international adoption can generate."

"We'll all be anxious to hear about your trip," Paul told her. Everyone nodded in agreement and broke out into little side conversations. Jolene and Brita were talking about the difficulty of learning Korean. Carla and Gina were encouraging each other.

Paul looked over at me. "Okay, Patrish. Now it's your turn to tell us what brought you here tonight."

I pursed my lips, sat up straight, and launched into my story. My face grew hot and turned red. All eyes were focused on me. I told them the beginning of the story right up to the current situation of waiting to hear from Katie. I slumped back and looked into each face.

"That's quite a story," Jolene stated with an understanding nod.

Paul grinned. "We encourage people to say as much as they feel comfortable sharing and try to keep the comments positive. You told us you came here because you're having trouble handling your birth mother's rejection and reaction to you. What do you think you'd like to do next?"

"I have no clue. I was hoping to find help here. My birth mom doesn't seem to want contact from me. I'd be happy to have a relationship with Katie, but Nora is who I really want to meet."

"When my son contacted me, he used an unusual approach you might want to try," Brita added. "He sent me a letter telling me about himself and his family. He included a self-addressed return envelope and his picture. He stated if I didn't want any contact with him, I should send the picture back in the envelope. It would be the signal I had no interest in a reunion. He asked me to include any medical history from my side of the family. Of course, I was thrilled to hear from him and ready to welcome him into my family. I didn't need to send the picture back."

I grimaced. "Writing the letter would be a big step for me. I don't know if I'd be able to handle getting my picture sent back. I'm still reeling from the rejection."

Paul leaned toward me. "I like the idea of a letter. You can express your feelings and tell her about your family. Grandchildren add an extra layer. You caught her off guard. Getting a private letter might help her. She's also had time to think about the situation since you contacted her a couple of weeks ago."

Jolene nodded. "I think you should send the letter and picture. The concern here would be her husband opening it. They're another generation. Maybe he goes through all the mail, or he might ask her about the letter she's opening. That's why I haven't sent one to my birth mother."

"Can you imagine how angry she'd be if all three of her family members found out this secret?" I asked in a shaky voice. "It's bad enough I'm going through Katie and her granddaughter Janine. Adding her husband to the list might freak her out."

Roberto said, "You can't be responsible for the way she feels. She needs to learn to deal with this the best way she can. This is hard for you right now but look on the bright side. You might gain a relationship with your half sister. Later, maybe a chance to get to know your birth mom."

I pulled my shoulders back. "I will write the letter, but I'll need to think about the picture and return envelope."

"It's a big step for you. You'll have to let us know how it went at the next meeting," Paul said. "Okay everyone, it's nine o'clock. If you would help put the chairs back at the tables, I'd appreciate it."

Brita approached me. "Don't get intimidated by your birth mother. Stay positive."

"Thank you, Brita. Your perspective on this is important to me."

After she left, Jolene came over. "We have similar stories. Hang in there. I'll be anxious to hear how the letter goes."

"This meeting has been so good for me. I feel empowered. It might take a while to figure out what to say to her, but I want to send the letter. Maybe next time, I can hear more of your story."

"We'll talk then. Good night, Patrish."

The stories I heard tonight played through my head all the way home. What would I say in the letter? Brent greeted me when I walked into the living room.

"How did it go? Were they supportive?"

"It's a wonderful group of people. Honest, willing to share. I'm amazed at the stories I heard. Yes, they were very helpful," I answered.

"But…"

"They suggested I write Nora a letter. Tell her about myself, our family." I waved my hands in the air. "I don't know how much to say or how to word it. She's not receptive to me. I'll think about it tonight and at least make a draft tomorrow."

I told him about the picture and the return envelope.

He pulled me into a hug. "It's worth a try. She's had time to come to terms that you're looking for her."

I returned his hug and relaxed in his arms. Tomorrow's another day.

CHAPTER ELEVEN

I woke up early, went into the kitchen, and made a hot cup of tea. The sky was still black, and the quiet house seemed perfect for starting the letter.

I wanted to do this the old fashion way. I took my tea, pencil, pad of paper, and walked into the living room. The comfy couch beckoned me. I plopped down and tapped the pencil against my cheek. Where to start.

I should be factual, confident, yet empathetic, making it clear my adoptive parents are wonderful. I wanted to open a door for her to enter if she chooses to. Hmmm. I doodled on the paper, then got to the message.

I had the letter completed when I heard the kids getting ready for school, and Brent getting cereal for breakfast. I rose from the couch when Nate and Hayley came into the living room.

"You're an early bird," said Hayley. "Who's taking us to school today?"

"I can. Don't forget your books in the den, Nate." I looked at Hayley. "I put your new notebook on the bar in the kitchen. Get some breakfast, and I'll get ready to take you."

Brent had an early meeting and left when we did.

"Good luck with the letter. I'd like to hear the final draft tonight."

"You will. It still needs some tweaking." I wrinkled my forehead. "Where this will lead, no one knows."

Back home, I got my stationery out of the desk drawer. Time to make this official.

Dear Mrs. Bower,

My name is Patrish. My birthday is November 5. You know who I am. Please read this letter all the way through. I'm not trying to invade your life. What I want to do is thank you for the hard decision you made. It led to a wonderful life for me. I was raised by loving parents and grew up in an affluent part of San Diego. I went to a private high school and graduated from San Diego State University. I love traveling and have been fortunate to see most of the US, as well as Europe.

Two people who called me their daughter fulfilled your desire for me to have all the things a child would need. I've been married for twenty-two years. Brent and I have two children. Hayley is sixteen, and Nate is thirteen. We have a comfortable life.

I'm telling you this to give you an idea of who I am and to thank you for wanting the best for me. I would also like to apologize for upsetting you. I have wanted to contact you for years, and it took me this long to finally reach out. It's natural for me to be curious about you and your life. I had hoped the feeling would be mutual.

I would like to hear from you and open a door of communication, even if it's only a small door. I'm leaving it up to you. I'll give you my address, phone number, and email. I've enclosed a recent picture of myself.

If you don't want any contact, I'll try to understand and view things from your perspective. I was disheartened you weren't open to getting to know me. Enclosed is a return envelope. If you decide you don't want any further contact, send my picture back. It will let me know how you feel. Please consider this carefully. I'd appreciate you including any family medical history you can give me.

I hope this contact will turn out to be a positive move for both of us.

Sincerely, Patrish.

My head fell back as I looked upward. *Please God, soften her heart.*

Getting all the contents together, I put a stamp on the envelope and, with trembling hands, put it in the mailbox. I crossed my fingers. Who would I hear from first, Katie or Nora? Maybe neither. A new waiting game commenced.

That evening, I handed the copy of my final draft to Brent. I held my breath, waiting for his response.

"It's good, Patrish, it gives her an idea of who you are and what you've done. It sounds hopeful without being heavy-handed. I like it." He handed it back to me.

"It's out of my control now. I hope she's able to read the letter before her husband intercepts it."

One week later, I walked out to the mailbox and gasped.

"No, no, no. This can't be."

I closed my eyes and forced back the tears. There was the envelope. My handwriting. I opened my eyes and took a closer look. It turned out to be the original letter I had sent. I had two addresses for her and decided to send it to the post office box first. It appeared the box number no longer existed, so the letter came back to me.

I leaned against the mailbox, trying to settle my wild, beating heart. False alarm. She hadn't even received it yet. I shook my head as the adrenaline rush receded. What a close call. Now, I needed to send it to the house address and wait.

Two days passed, and I had a crazy idea.

"Brent." I slowly walked over to the computer where he sat checking emails. "How do you feel about taking a one-day road trip?"

"What do you have in mind?"

"I wondered about going to Palm Desert."

"You mean to see where Nora lives?"

"I don't want to seem like I'm stalking her, but my curiosity is piqued to see what her life is like now."

He raised his eyebrows. "To do what? Ring her doorbell?"

"No, that would be too bold. If she hasn't told her husband about me, I don't want to give him a heart attack or have the door slammed in my face. Maybe we could drive to the house, find a place to sit in the car, and watch it for a while. I don't know how it will work. I want to check out the community where she lives and see what she sees every day. I hope it doesn't sound creepy. It feels weird even saying it. Who knows, maybe she'll come outside to go to the store or water plants. It might be my chance to see her."

Brent laughed. He stood, shook his head, and gave me a hug.

"Not creepy, but a little crazy. It's not a bad idea. Palm Desert is only a two-hour drive. Do you know where her house is?"

"Yes, I looked it up on the computer. The website for the community says there's a gate and a guardhouse. We'll have to figure out a way to get through without Nora knowing I'm there."

"When do you want to go?"

"Do you think you can spare time on Tuesday? We'll want to avoid driving in awful traffic. Maybe we could leave around nine in the morning. We'll stay as long as we feel we need to."

"Okay, I'll keep Tuesday open."

"Thank you for understanding. This whole thing has thrown me for a loop. I guess I keep looking for ways to make it turn out better."

Before I knew it, Tuesday was here. My twitchy stomach made eating breakfast impossible. With my mind a million miles away,

I managed to get the kids to school. Arriving at home, Brent had dressed and backed his car out of the garage.

"Today's the big day," he declared. "How do you feel?"

I held up my shaking hands. "Does this answer your question? I still want to go, though. I guess we'll see what happens."

On the drive to Palm Springs, I was lost in thought. I glanced at the clock every fifteen minutes, hope and dread vying for equal time. I put on a Josh Groban CD, surrounding myself with his powerful voice and beautiful lyrics.

Brent allowed me this quiet time. When we got close to Palm Desert, he asked me which exit to take. I gave him directions off the freeway and on the side roads to Nora's community.

"We need to figure out what we're going to say to the guards, so they'll let us in the gate," said Brent.

I nodded. "I have an idea. Play along with me."

Driving up to the gate, the guard said, "Who are you here to see?"

I leaned over toward Brent and gave the guard a charming smile. "We wanted to come in and see the community. My mom's thinking about moving here, and we'd like to check it out for her."

"You can't come in unless you know a resident," he replied.

"We want to see if it suits her. Can we come in and take a short drive around?"

Brent and I continued to smile.

After a pause, he replied, "I'll give you a pass to go to the Community Center. It's the only place you can stop. Here's a map. Follow it straight ahead."

"Thank you," Brent and I commented together, waving as we passed through the gate.

We smiled smugly at our first success.

The first obstacle was removed, now to find her house. I knew what street she lived on and located it on the map. We drove straight, saw the Community Center, and zipped right past it. We turned left on her street and saw her house halfway down the block.

I surveyed the neighborhood. "This is a pleasant area and on the golf course. Look Brent, someone's home. There's a car in the driveway."

We parked across the street. "What do we do now?" asked Brent.

I folded my arms. "I've never done anything like this before. It makes me feel closer to her seeing where she lives, where she drives every day. I guess I'm hoping to see her come out." I laughed. "Can you imagine her coming out, driving to the grocery store, us following her, and we end up face-to-face with only a shopping cart between us?"

Brent's eyes widened. "I'd like to see that reaction."

"I'm not brave enough to ring the doorbell. What if Ross answered? Maybe I look like her, and he'd keel over. This is between Nora and me. It's up to her whether she tells him."

"We can sit here for a while."

An hour later, we were squirming in our seats. I rubbed my back, and Brent rubbed his neck.

"Let's go to the Community Center restaurant for lunch," said Brent. "All this sitting still is making me stiff."

"Sounds good. We can eat and use the bathroom."

Brent ordered a turkey sandwich with chips, and I ordered a chef salad.

He leaned forward. "Look around the room. Maybe she's here having lunch, too."

"What a kick that would be." I laughed, gazing around the room. "I don't see anyone matching her description."

Brent looked around. "She could come for lunch or meet her friends here. Watch the door. She could come through it at any minute."

"You have a vivid imagination. I'll keep a lookout. This would be a great way to see her."

We finished and pushed back our chairs. I picked up my purse. "No Nora. Let's go back to her neighborhood for a little while longer."

When we got to her house, I pointed to the driveway. "Look, there's a new car parked there."

"Maybe she'll come out now."

Brent closed his eyes while I kept mine focused on the front door. It was a warm day, and we had the windows down to let the light breeze in. Not a single car drove down the street. There were a few golfers on the course, and we could hear the whack of their clubs hitting the balls.

The front door of Nora's house opened. Brent opened his eyes as two people emerged.

The street was so narrow we could hear everything they said, even though they weren't shouting.

"Thank you, Mr. Bower. My mom will love this plant clipping you gave me. She has a green thumb. It'll be thriving in no time," remarked a petite blonde. She got into the car parked in the driveway.

"You're welcome, Sabrina. Say hi to her and your dad for me," he said and turned back into the house.

I let out a loud sigh and rubbed my hands on my pants. "Okay, we saw Ross, but not Nora. Dang."

"Disappointing. Too bad Nora didn't come out, too."

I put my hand on his arm. "I think we're done here. It's time to go home. At least we saw Ross and know we had the right house. Thank you for indulging me, Brent. It hasn't been exciting for you."

I closed my eyes on the ride home, blocking out the world. I opened them every once in a while to make sure Brent wasn't sleepy. We really hadn't accomplished anything. At least not what I'd hoped. How much longer would I have to wait to hear from Fact Finders?

It was 6:15 a.m., Monday, May 2, when I got my email answer from Eric.

> Please call me as soon as you get this message. I got a call, and it's not good news.

CHAPTER TWELVE

I moaned. "What now?"

No one was up yet. My words filled the quiet room, and panic clawed at my throat. I put my hands on my neck and tried to suppress the panic with big gulps of breath.

My feet felt glued to the carpet. I looked over at the phone, eyeing it as if it were a snake coiled and ready to strike. Picking up a pen and paper, I cautiously made my way to the phone.

I dialed Eric's number and closed my eyes as it rang.

I jumped when he answered.

"Hi, Patrish. A message was left on our phone from Jay Hughes. He said he represented the Bower family, and they want nothing to do with the person looking for information. There is to be no contact made to the Bower family by phone or writing." His tone softened. "He didn't say he represented them as their attorney, although that is the impression he gave. I am so sorry your search took this detour."

I covered my mouth, trying to suppress the sob that escaped. I cleared my throat. "This has turned into a nightmare. Total and complete rejection by the whole family. I can't even think straight. I'm devastated."

I wrote thirteen words on my blank sheet of paper.

Message left from someone representing Bowers—Jay Hughes—
no solicitation, phone, or writing.

"We were shocked at their reaction, too. Rita wanted me to reaffirm to you not to take it personally. They don't know you. Nora needed to protect herself."

I clutched the phone with my left hand, and I put my right hand over my heart. My voice rose a full octave.

"It feels personal, like a stab to my heart. Most of my adopted friends had decent reunions. Now, I'll never know anything about my background. It's more than I can take," I wailed, sagging back into the chair.

"We know this is a difficult time for you." He was obviously choosing his words with great care. "As a company, we can't pursue this any further. In a week, you should receive the entire report. It will include our research process, the conversation between Nora and Rita, and all the family information we obtained."

I let out a humorless laugh. "I don't know what good it will do, but at least it's something. Except they're only words on paper. I wanted to see her face-to-face. Look her in the eyes and maybe get a smile and a hug. I'm heartbroken that she doesn't feel the same way."

Eric's voice echoed my concerns. "It's not often we have to give someone bad news. Maybe she'll be more receptive in the future. Her secret is out. Katie or Janine might still want to know more about you."

My voice cracked. "Thank you for your support. Please thank Rita for me, too."

"I will. We all wish you the best in the future."

Nine weeks on the merry-go-round, and we were done. I laid my head on my arms and sobbed. Loud, gasping, aching cries.

Brent heard my distress and ran into the kitchen. He sat in the chair next to me, rubbing my back.

"Oh, Patrish, you called Eric? What happened?"

I lifted my head. It felt like it weighed a ton. I tried to find my voice. It came out as a croak.

"Nora wiped me out of her family. A firm no, without hesitation."

I repeated what Eric had told me. I stood, wiping my tear-stained cheeks.

Brent reached out and pulled me into a firm embrace. "Wow, that's cold. Her reaction has been to run, protect herself. I'm proud of you for hanging in there and seeing this through. Eric's right, maybe this isn't the end. You have their info. Maybe later you'll feel like pursuing it."

I tightened the embrace, rubbing his back as he rubbed mine. I could hear Hayley and Nate getting ready for school.

"I'm shaken by all this, Brent. Will you give them breakfast and take them to school?"

"Yes," he replied. Stepping back, he took my hands. "Whatever you need, I'm here for you."

I gave him a weak smile and went to the bedroom. I sat on the bed trembling, rocking back and forth. I kept my eyes closed and listened to the kids in the other room.

"Mom, are you okay?" Hayley asked. "Your eyes are red and puffy."

I opened my eyes to my kids staring at me.

"I will be. I had a disturbing phone call," I whispered, looking down at my hands. "I'll tell you about it after school. Dad's going to take you today."

Hayley gave me a hug and went back to her room.

"Don't forget, we need more copy paper, so I can finish my history report," said Nate, watching me closely.

I grabbed a tissue and tried to smile. "It'll be there when you need it."

Brent called, "Come on, grab your stuff for school." He turned to me. "I'll go right to the office after dropping them off. Are you all right?"

I looked at him through glazed eyes. "No, I'm not. I'm trying to process all this, but I feel numb. I want to smile and be cheerful in front of the kids. I can't move from this spot. Go ahead and take the kids and go to the office. I'll work through it."

"Call me if you need anything," he whispered, and gave me a soft kiss.

The quiet house provided solace. I sank into my favorite blue recliner and pulled my knees up to my chin. The excitement I'd experienced in the early stages of the search seemed distant. What had I said back then? The journey of a lifetime. A momentous occasion. No turning back, come what may. All true, but not the results I wanted.

I stared out the window at a beautiful, sunny day. I could hear birds chirping, a lawn mower rumbling, and cars driving down our street. Life went on for everyone else. My gloomy spirit belonged only to me.

I stood and wandered around the house. The kids' laundry baskets were full, a fine layer of dust covered the coffee table in the living room, and the morning dishes were in the sink.

"Not right now," I muttered under my breath. I decided going outside for a walk might help distract me from the chores I didn't want to do.

Walking up and down the hills in our neighborhood invigorated me. I kept a steady, slow pace. Not my usual exercise level, but right now, I was pleased I could move at all. It provided good thinking time. Where do I go from here? I have all the family info. I could still call her, even though she wanted no contact. I knew I had to let this whole thing cool down before I did anything else.

An hour later, I tackled the chores I'd put off. I started with Nate's laundry, sorting the colors and putting a load in the washing machine. Next came the breakfast dishes. I cleaned off the counters and dusted the table. On a roll now, I vacuumed and picked up scattered piles of mail left around the house.

Cleaning proved therapeutic.

I picked the kids up from school.

"You look better, Mom," said Hayley.

I turned to look over at her in the passenger seat.

"I feel better, but I can't help but be sad. The entire search process ended today after an early morning phone call. My birth mother told me not to contact her or anyone in her family ever again. I'm taking it hard."

When we got home, Hayley said, "I'll make dinner tonight, Mom." Hayley sounded like a grown-up when she said to her brother, "Nate, we'd better pick up our rooms. Mom cleaned the house, so let's give her a break."

I smiled at my sweet sixteen-year-old. "Dinner's easy tonight. Cheeseburger pie and salad. Thank you for helping."

At six o'clock, we heard the garage door open.

Brent glided into the kitchen with his hand behind his back.

"I have a surprise for you, Patrish." In his hand, he held a beautiful array of red, white, and yellow roses.

"Oh, Brent," I squealed, spreading my hands wide to accept my gift. "They're gorgeous, and they smell wonderful. Thank you for cheering me up."

I handed the roses to Hayley and threw my arms around his neck. Our tender kiss expressed my love and appreciation.

Hayley handed the roses back to me, opened the oven, and pulled dinner out.

Brent moved closer to the oven, inhaling the smell of melted cheese. "You made dinner tonight? Looks good. Thanks for helping Mom. I noticed the house and your rooms are clean. Did you do that, too?" He wiggled his eyebrows.

Nate came into the kitchen grinning. "Mom cleaned the house, so we cleaned our rooms. Hayley was right. She needed a break."

"Good job, you two. She seems like she feels better."

"These roses need water. Nate, will you help Hayley get the food on the table?" I reached up to get a vase out of the cupboard. I cut the stems, put water in the vase, and arranged them. I positioned the vase on the counter.

"They do make me feel better, Brent. This morning was horrible, but you guys helped it turn out okay." I smiled at all of them. "Let's eat."

CHAPTER THIRTEEN

Two days later at dinner, Brent said, "Don't forget. Saturday night we're meeting my family in Little Italy to celebrate my sister's birthday."

"Thanks for reminding me. I'm not good company right now, but I don't want to miss Danielle's birthday. I can count my blessings; your family is always supportive. I'll put on a happy face."

Jackie is the only one I had talked to about the results of my search. I was still experiencing highs and lows, constantly recapping everything in my head.

We arrived at the quaint Italian restaurant to find everyone already seated and in high spirits.

"Hi, everyone!" I exclaimed, making my way around the table to embrace Danielle and give her a birthday card. "Happy birthday. We're so happy to see you all."

Danielle sat at the head of the table and had an array of cards next to her water glass and balloons tied to her chair.

Jackie and her daughter, Vanessa, were on Danielle's right, leaning in together laughing at an old photo Jackie brought of Danielle on her thirteenth birthday.

"Glad you could make it." Jackie beamed. "Come sit next to us." She pointed to the seat by her son. "Nate, we saved you a seat by Ryan."

"Hi, Michaela," I said to Danielle's daughter, taking a seat beside her. "We haven't seen you in a while."

"It takes a birthday to get us all together," said Kevin, Danielle's husband.

The waiter came over to take our drink orders as Brent sat at the end of the table, Hayley on his right.

"Acqua fredda per tutti?" he asked in his best Italian accent.

I laughed. "If you mean water for everyone, the answer is yes."

"Grazie." He bowed and moved on to take Danielle's cocktail order.

Huddling in together, Brent asked Hayley and Nate what they'd like to order. Brent decided on his favorite fettuccine Alfredo. I wanted the spaghetti, Nate and Hayley chose the pasta shells with marinara sauce.

"Looks like a good crowd here tonight," I said to Jackie. "I'm having trouble hearing Kevin and Danielle at the other end of the table."

"What?" she yelled for effect and laughed. "It's loud in here. That table over to the right has a large group like ours, and they're boisterous. Here comes our waiter again."

"Buona sera. My name is Antonio. What may I get for you?"

We ordered our food, and Antonio moved around the table, taking all the orders, while servers placed water, bread, and olive oil before us.

Hayley started giggling, drawing all of our table's attention.

"What are you laughing at?" Nate inquired.

"Look at that kid sitting at the big table. He's trying to balance a spoon on his nose," she said, pointing to the other large group.

We all turned our heads to see the spectacle.

"I can't believe he kept it up there for so long. His little brother is trying to copy him. The little guy must be about four years old, but he hasn't mastered it yet." Michaela chuckled.

Kevin cleared his throat and announced in a loud voice, "Okay, attention please." He turned to Danielle. "It's time for my beautiful wife to open her birthday cards."

Danielle beamed. A few cards were sentimental, others were funny and referred to her *old age.*

She looked right at Vanessa. "Ha, ha. Before you know it, you'll be fifty-eight, too. It goes by fast, and it's not old." She laughed. "I'm a classic."

"Let's not project my daughter's age out that far," Jackie protested. "When she's fifty-eight, I'll be seventy-seven." She grimaced.

We all roared with laughter. Brent and I exchanged knowing looks. That age was around the corner for us, too.

Jackie looked over at me. "How are you doing, Patrish? You must still be in shock."

My eyes watered. "I am. It still hurts, and Mother's Day is tomorrow. We'll spend it with my mom, but Nora will be on my mind. I didn't expect such a strong, negative reaction from her. I might have ruined her Mother's Day, too."

Michaela turned toward me. "Jackie told us what happened. I know you had a hundred things you wanted to tell her. I got you this as a Mother's Day gift." She handed me a book full of heartfelt letters daughters wrote to their moms.

"I saw it and thought of you. Maybe it'll inspire you to write her a letter from your heart, telling her how you feel. God has a plan for you, your birth mother, and half sister."

My voice was thick with emotion. "Thank you, Michaela. This is a wonderful gift. I'm still a little raw from it all, but it'll get better over time. Maybe then I can write to her again."

Those close around must have heard because Jackie said, "Yes, it will!"

"I'll toast to that," said Michaela, and they all raised their glasses.

I leaned over and gave her a hug and blew them all a kiss.

Brent smiled. "Nora's the loser here. This is not the outcome I was hoping for you."

"There's still time for her to change her mind," said Jackie. "It's not a closed door, only a swinging one."

"Thank you all for caring about me."

The air filled with the wonderful scent of roasted tomatoes and cheese. Our dinner was served with great fanfare, as we all oohed and awed.

"This looks delicious." I swirled my spaghetti and took a bite. "Oh, I was right, delizioso."

"How do you like your shells?" Brent asked Hayley and Nate.

They both gave him a thumbs up.

Antonio appeared. "Is everything to your liking?"

Our mouths were all full, so we nodded.

"Buon appetito," he said, bowing.

Brent laughed. "He's a character. I love the Italian phrases. Makes the atmosphere more authentic."

"How's your food?" Danielle asked in a loud voice.

Brent raised his fork twirled with fettuccine. "Superb. How about yours? We can't hear your end of the conversation from way down here."

"My chicken parm is exquisite," she answered. "Vanessa's keeping us entertained with antics from work."

"Never a dull moment," Vanessa exclaimed.

Ryan dipped a piece of bread in the olive oil and popped it into his mouth. "My spaghetti is good, too. A little different from the one you make, Mom."

"There are hundreds of recipes for it. Somehow it tastes better when someone else makes it," said Jackie.

After eating half my meal, I put my fork down. "I'm done. The leftovers will taste wonderful tomorrow."

"I'm done, too," said Hayley. "We'll need to take home containers."

"Nate and I will finish ours." Brent took another bite.

Kevin whispered something to the busboy, who took his empty plate. With a knowing nod, he rushed off.

Take home containers were distributed, and the plates were cleared. Kevin motioned to us and pointed straight ahead.

"Attention please. A surprise for the birthday girl."

We all turned to see Antonio carrying what appeared to be a tray filled with sparklers. He set it in front of Danielle. Her jaw dropped at the impressive tiramisu cake covered in sparkler candles.

Kevin started singing happy birthday, and we, along with others in the restaurant, joined in.

Danielle beamed. "Thank you," and blew out the candles.

Antonio handed her a large knife to cut the cake and said, "Buon compleanno, signora."

I looked at Brent and put my hand on his arm. In a soft voice, I confided, "This has been a great night. I love it when we all get together. It might be Danielle's birthday, but I needed this, too."

"We lean on family in difficult times; that's what they're there for. I'm glad you feel better."

Michaela passed out the cake, and the bill arrived. We looked over the charges, adding up our portion. The whole family had decided to split up Danielle's share of the check, so we added it to ours.

Money piled up in the center of the table. Vanessa counted it to make sure we left enough for a tip. Standing, we gave goodbye hugs to everyone.

"Don't forget your leftovers," I said.

Hayley, Vanessa, Jackie, and Michaela lifted theirs for me to see.

Outside, the crisp air filled our lungs. I took a deep breath and sighed.

Hayley climbed into our car. "That was fun."

"Your side of the family is fun," Nate said to Dad. "Not to say your side isn't, Mom."

I laughed. "Tomorrow we'll spend the day with Grandma. It will seem quiet after tonight."

Chapter Fourteen

I was up before the sun on Mother's Day. The darkness enveloped me like a warm blanket. I sat on the couch, thinking about Nora. What would her Mother's Day be like? She most likely wouldn't spend it with Katie since they lived far apart. I hope I didn't ruin their relationship by revealing Nora's secret.

I let out a soulful sigh, sipped my tea, and let my mind drift back to happier days when I thought I might get to meet her.

About forty-five minutes later, I heard Brent get up. He ambled into the room and sat beside me on the couch. "You're up early. I'm guessing you're thinking about Nora."

We sat in silence for a few seconds, then Brent said, "I wonder what Katie and Janine are thinking. It must be strange for them."

"It probably is. For me, every day is different. I'm up, down, sad, okay. All over the place."

I put my feet on the couch and pulled my knees up to my chin. "The good part is we get to celebrate Mother's Day with Mom. I haven't told her all the results yet. I don't want to ruin her day, but I think I can be objective when I tell her. I don't want her to think Nora is more important to me than she is."

Brent put his hand on my knee, keeping his other hand hidden behind his back. "She knows how you feel about her. That's why she's been encouraging you through your search. Here's your Mother's Day present."

He pulled his hand from behind his back and handed me a small red box.

I opened it carefully and saw a beautiful silver necklace with a heart in the center.

He spoke in a tender and sweet voice. "You're the heart of this family, and you have my heart. Happy Mother's Day, Patrish. I love you."

We stood together, and I put my arms around his neck. I could smell his aftershave and fingered his hair. His lips were soft as we kissed, and his hands pressed against my back. The sun poured through the windows, and I heard birds singing.

"I love you, too," I whispered. "The necklace is gorgeous. Thank you." We stood in an embrace for a few more seconds before stepping apart.

I smiled at him. "Time to get the kids up and get ready for church. I'll need your help to fasten my necklace after I get dressed."

I strode down the hall toward the kids' rooms and heard a chorus of "Happy Mother's Day!"

Two grinning faces appeared, and Hayley ran to me. She threw her arms around my neck, holding on tight.

"I love you, Mom." I held her close, loving the familiar smell of her hair, the touch of her soft skin.

I let go and turned to Nate. He put his arms around my waist. I put my chin on his head and hugged him, swaying from side to side, kissing his head before stepping back.

"You guys give the best hugs."

We all hugged again.

"Okay,"—I laughed—"time to get ready for church. What do you want for breakfast?"

Brent came out of the bedroom. "I'm ready to go. I'll make noodles and eggs for you. Mom shouldn't have to cook on Mother's Day."

"Thanks. It'll give me more time to get ready."

I could hear Nate rummaging through his dresser drawers and Hayley picking through her closet. The aroma of cooking noodles filled the house. I hummed as I chose a simple blouse to wear. I wanted something that would show off the heart necklace.

Brent had finished cooking breakfast, and Hayley helped set the table. I showed Hayley the box with my new necklace.

"Look what Dad got me for Mother's Day," I said, my eyes shining.

Brent came over to fasten it around my neck.

"A heart, Dad, that's beautiful," Hayley said. She leaned closer to get a better view.

"Cool, Dad. Looks like Mom loves it," Nate added.

"We have cards for you, Mom. They're here on the table." Hayley pointed to my chair. Two sparkling cards were next to my silverware.

"Grab a plate. We don't want to be late for church," Brent reminded us.

I read each of the cards. "These are perfect. Thank you."

"What time is Grandma coming?" Hayley asked, holding a fork filled with noodles and eggs.

"She'll be here at three. We'll straighten the house after church and start prepping for dinner. Make sure your rooms are clean."

"I'm done," Nate announced. "All I have to do is brush my teeth."

Brent and I finished and took our plates to the kitchen. Hayley took her last bite and helped clear the glasses off the table.

After finishing last-minute details, we drove to church. The kids went to their respective classes, and we sat in the sanctuary. Creatures of habit, we sat in the same area every Sunday. We greeted our church friends, and the worship songs began. I love singing in church. It fills my soul. The message centered on mothers, reminding us of the influence they have on their children's lives and their homes. He cited Proverbs 31: 10-12 "A wife of noble character who can find? She is worth far more than rubies. Her husband has full confidence in her and lacks nothing of value. She brings him good, not harm, all the days of her life."

Big shoes to fill.

Every woman received a red rose after the services. When we pulled into the driveway, there was a floral arrangement on our doorstep. I looked at Brent.

Shrugging, he said, "They're not from me."

Brent waited for us to get out of the car, and then he pulled it into the garage. Hayley ran up to the front door.

"They're for you, Mom. But we didn't send them. Here's the card."

I read it out loud. "From the family who loves you. Happy Mother's Day. Love, Jackie, Ryan, and Vanessa."

My voice caught in my throat. "How sweet and thoughtful. Look at the beautiful colors in this bouquet." There were pink peonies, yellow tulips, white and purple Peruvian lilies, baby's breath, and greenery.

"They want to make you feel better after what happened with your birth mom," Nate stated.

"It worked. Let's take these inside."

I unlocked the door and carried the arrangement into the dining room.

"It'll have a place of honor right here in the middle of the table. Okay, everyone, change clothes and let's get ready for Grandma to come over."

Brent came in through the garage at the same time we entered the house. He saw the flowers and read the card.

"They love and appreciate you, Patrish. The flowers look great on the table."

After everyone changed into casual attire, we gathered in the kitchen.

"Okay, here's what I'd like you to do. Nate, please straighten the living room. Hayley, set the table. It's gloomy outside, so we'll eat in here. Brent, start marinating the steaks and make the hamburger patties. I'll chop cabbage for the coleslaw and cut up tomatoes for the hamburgers."

They smiled, gave me a mock salute, and began their duties.

Mom arrived on time with her delicious potato salad. I greeted her at the door with a hug.

"Happy Mother's Day. I'll carry it for you." I took the bowl from her, and she followed me to the refrigerator. "Thank you for making it. Your potato salad is the only one Hayley and I will eat. What is your secret ingredient, anyway? I haven't been able to duplicate it."

She set her purse on the floor by the computer. "I use a lot of mayonnaise and cook the small, yellow potatoes until they get soft. That's it."

"Oops, I use the baking potatoes. That must be where I go wrong."

Mom glanced over at our food preparations. "I'm looking forward to dinner. Where are Hayley and Nate?"

"Here we are!" they announced, rushing from their rooms.

Mom pulled them into a three-way hug, rocking them back and forth.

Glancing at the table, Mom said, "You have a pretty flower arrangement. Are they from Brent?"

"No. Brent gave me this necklace." I held the necklace away from my neck to give her a better look. "The flowers are from Jackie and her family. We went to dinner last night for Danielle's birthday."

"I like the pretty necklace, Brent," said Mom. "Did you have a good time last night?"

"Yes, it was fun. I want to tell you why they gave me flowers." I told her about my conversation with Fact Finders and how it all ended.

"Oh my," she said, taking me into her arms. "What a harsh way to finish. This has been so important to you. It's not fair for them to have the final say on it."

"They must have been shocked when I reached out. I hope it didn't ruin Mother's Day for Nora."

"I'd like to see your notes and the information you've collected from Fact Finders," said Mom.

I brought out my notes, and Brent went to the patio to turn on the grill. As Mom read what I'd written, I helped Brent carry the hamburgers and steaks outside.

"When will you get the complete report?" Mom asked as I came through the door from the patio.

"It should be sometime this week. Then I'll know all the specifics."

Nate and Hayley came back into the dining room.

"Grandma, here's your Mother's Day card." Hayley handed her a bright pink envelope.

"Here's the one from me." Nate placed a white envelope on the table.

"Thank you." She unsealed Hayley's first to find a glittery card filled with loving sentiments.

"This card is beautiful, Hayley. I'll treasure it. Okay, Nate, let's read yours."

The outside of the card featured balloons, and the inside read, "To the best Grandma ever."

"Thank you, I love it. Come here, you two. It's time for another hug."

They each went over to her and gave her a gentle, sincere hug. I placed her cards at the head of the table.

I handed her a card from Brent and me. "We have one for you, too."

"Oh, this is fancy. It has a bookmark inside." A tear shone in the corner of her eye. "I'm not sure I live up to all the things this card says, but thank you."

I bent down and kissed her on the cheek.

"Here's the food," Brent exclaimed, coming through the patio door carrying a large, sizzling tray. The savory aroma of beef filled the room.

I went to the refrigerator and got out the coleslaw and potato salad. Next came the pickles, tomatoes, lettuce, ketchup, and mustard. The hamburger buns were on a platter. Hayley helped me set everything on the counter next to the meat for a serve yourself buffet.

"Mom, you go first," I told her. "You can sit where we put your cards."

Brent, Mom, and I chose the steak. Hayley and Nate picked hamburgers. Everyone wanted a scoop of potato salad and coleslaw.

After filling our plates and finding our seats, Brent prayed a blessing over the food, adding a special blessing for Mom and me.

Mom took a bite of steak. "This is delicious, Brent. It's cooked the way I like it." She turned to me. "Getting back to Nora, Patrish. You have no way of knowing what happened when she had to tell Katie about you." Her features softened, and she looked directly into my eyes. "It might not have been the confrontation you've seen in your mind. Maybe Katie will seek you out on her own."

"I've asked myself the same question," I said, putting down my fork. "Talking to Katie would be a perfect way to learn about Nora. Fact Finders didn't give me an address or phone number for Katie or her daughter, Janine. I suppose Katie could find a way to contact me. Nora may have thrown away my letter and the letter Eric sent to Katie. She'd have to do the research herself without telling her mom."

"Have you tried looking on the computer? Now that you know her name, you might be able to find her."

Brent and Nate listened to our conversation, looking back and forth between us as they took bites of dinner.

"I did look it up, but no address was listed. Only her name as a connection to Ross and Nora. I'm going to sit on this for a while. Process it through my mind and emotions."

"Let me know if there's anything I can do," said Mom.

We ate in silence for a few minutes. Hayley cleared her throat.

"I have some mom jokes," Hayley said, setting down her hamburger and smiling. "Why did the cookie cry? Because his mother was a wafer so long."

We all laughed.

"I have more. What flowers are best for Mother's Day? Mums.

What sweets do astronauts' moms like? Mars bars."

"They're cute." I smiled at her and at my mom's big grin.

"Where did you get all these jokes?" asked Brent.

"I heard them at school on Friday."

"Thanks for the comic relief." Mom chuckled. "Do you have any jokes, Nate?"

"Nope, not a one," he confessed, and shook his head.

I covered my mouth. We started laughing again. "I can't finish my steak if we keep joking around. I might choke."

"I'm all out of jokes now," Hayley informed us, swallowing the last bite of her hamburger. "And I'm done with my food. I'll take my plate to the kitchen. Anyone else finished?"

Brent waved his fork filled with potato salad. "This is my last bite. I'm going to savor it."

"I'm done, too, Hayley," I said, pointing to my plate. "Are you finished, Mom?"

"Yes. Nate looks done, too. Here's my plate, Hayley. The entire meal was excellent. Thank you for your great grilling skills, Brent."

We cleared the dishes and rinsed them in the sink.

"I have lemon cake for dessert. Let me know when you're ready. I'm too full to want it right now," I told them.

We sat in the living room for forty-five minutes, chatting about Nora and her family until Brent announced, "I'm ready for dessert."

I went to the kitchen, cut Mom a piece of cake, got her a cup of coffee, and placed it on the table. I cut cake for everyone, and we joined her.

"You know how much I love lemon, Patrish. Is this Mary's recipe from years ago? I love the tangy flavor," said Mom.

"Yes, it's her recipe. Hayley and I are lemon lovers, too. I think this is the best lemon cake recipe I've ever had."

After dessert, Mom was ready to leave.

"Thank you for a wonderful dinner and beautiful cards. What a perfect day."

"We're glad you came, Mom. It wouldn't be the same without you." I hugged her and patted her back.

We waved goodbye. Brent and I strolled back to the house arm in arm.

I smiled at Brent. "It was a good day today. The hamburgers and steaks were perfect."

"Thank you. You did the rest. I think your mom really enjoyed herself."

At night before bed, I prayed a thank you prayer.

"Thank you, God, for Your love and Your timing. Everything works out according to Your will. Thank you for my mom, Linnea Campbell, and her incredible capacity to love. Thank you for Brent, Hayley, and Nate. Thank you for Nora, Katie, and Janine, even if I never get to have a relationship with them. Thank you, Lord, for always watching out for me and my loved ones. In Jesus' name, Amen."

Chapter Fifteen

For the next few weeks, I found myself meandering from room to room, with no clear destination. My mind kept going back to the information I'd received from Fact Finders. I now knew everything they could find concerning the Bower family. It didn't make me feel better.

Thursday, June 16 rolled around, and I went to another Adoptee Awareness meeting.

My palms were sweaty on the steering wheel. I needed to tell them everything that had happened. Would I be able to get through it?

Inside the recreation center, I saw Paul arranging brochures again.

"Hi, Patrish. We're glad to see you came back."

"This is where I need to be. I've had a lot happen since the last meeting."

Chairs were once again placed in a circle. All the same people were there sitting in the same places as last time. I took my place and smiled at the group. I could hear small conversations and bursts of laughter.

"Okay, everyone, settle down," Paul said. "We'll skip introductions since we all know each other. Does anyone feel an urgent need to go first?"

I raised my hand. "If you don't mind, I'm having a hard time and would like to go first."

"Okay, Patrish, tell us what's going on."

I glanced around the room and cleared my throat. "You all helped me the last time. I followed your advice, Brita, and sent Nora a letter. I included a picture and a return, stamped envelope. At the same time, I'd been waiting to hear from my half sister, Katie, and her daughter. My husband and I even drove to Palm Desert. We found her house, saw her husband, but not Nora."

"What a bold move," Roberto affirmed. "Too bad you didn't see her. I'm lucky I have a relationship with both birth parents."

"I never rang the doorbell. We went there on April 26. Early in the morning on May 2, I got an email from Fact Finders asking me to call them." I explained the whole conversation.

"A flat out don't contact us?" Brad asked with raised eyebrows. "Wow, cold reaction. I never got to meet my birth parents, either."

Jolene frowned. "Eric was right. Nora probably had been trying to protect herself."

"I listened to you last month and your stories of reunions. I know not all of you had good ones, but this is the worst." My lips quivered and tears filled the corners of my eyes. "I never let myself think about how awful it would feel to be rejected. I had dreams of at least having a relationship with my half sister. Through her, I could learn about Nora, get pictures, maybe hear stories. To have the whole family say to leave them alone is unbearable."

Tears started flowing, and I put my hands on my head.

Jolene handed me a tissue. "It's hard to hear rejection. My birth mother told me nothing good would ever come from our having a relationship. I sympathize with your feeling hopeful. I still haven't met her. Made me wonder what happened in her life to make her bitter."

I blotted my eyes. "I wondered the same thing about Nora. I can imagine it must have scared her. The past came out of hiding and now everyone knows. My heart, though, still hurts."

"She must have read your letter," Brita stated. "You sent it before they called Fact Finders. I wonder if it influenced her at all. I read my son's letter right away."

"For all I know, she could have thrown it in the trash. Never looked at my picture or read it." I twisted my mouth. "I can't believe she wouldn't be a little bit curious about me. If it were me, I would have read it, even if I never planned on meeting in person."

Gina's expression grew serious. "Have you found out who this Jay Hughes guy is? Sounds like a lawyer but could've been anyone."

I glanced around the room and gave my head a vigorous shake. "No, I still don't know who he is. I wonder if her husband knew about me or if he found out with the others. It's a big secret to keep for fifty years. I had hoped Nora would feel a little relief at having her family know. Boy, how wrong could I be." I slumped in my chair.

"Fact Finders gave you all her information, right?" Paul asked. "Maybe there's still hope."

"Everyone says the same thing." My breath hitched. "I'm not ready to approach it for a while. Her reaction seemed mean spirited." My eyes filled with tears again. "I feel like I had a death in the family. The death of a little girl who only wanted to find out where she came from. My wish on my birthday every year, as I blew out the candles, was to see her face-to-face. I wondered if she ever thought about me on my special day or asked herself where life took me, or how I turned out. Guess I wasted too much time wishing."

I blew my nose and looked into eyes that mirrored my pain.

"Every birth mother has different circumstances," Brita pointed out. She leaned forward and looked right into my eyes.

"I did think about my son on his birthday. I wondered about all those things you mentioned. Don't let this define who you are. You were strong all along. The little girl inside you can stand up for herself."

"We all understand your anger and dismay," Jolene vocalized in a soft voice. "Her reaction stinks. No one deserves to be treated as though they don't exist. Brita's right. It's their loss. They don't even know you. We're here for you."

"Thank you all for your kind words and good advice. I'm glad I have a place to come to and vent. Sometimes I think I'd be better off leaving it alone. What an eye opener," I said, spreading my arms wide. "I appreciate the mom I grew up with even more now. Mother's Day turned out to be good this year, despite Nora's reaction. My mom understands the importance, and she knows it had nothing to do with our relationship. She got upset, too, when I told her what happened."

Paul went around the room and got an update from the rest of the group. After the meeting, Jolene rushed over to me.

She took my arm and whispered, "I'm sorry your search turned out this way. Hang in there, you'll be okay. Hearing you made me relive my horror story. I still shake my head in disbelief over my birth mother's reaction. But we are survivors."

"Thank you, Jolene. You above everyone else understand how I feel, and thank you for all the tissues," I said, emitting a small laugh.

CHAPTER SIXTEEN

I looked at my calendar. August 13, 2007. Hayley was nineteen now, and Nate had turned sixteen.

Two and a half years had passed since I started my search for Nora. Nothing more had happened. I had tried to call her number twice in that time, but she never answered.

Over the last few months, I had conducted periodic explorations on the computer, keeping tabs on her. I learned of a website where it listed a person's name, family members, and places they'd lived. I pulled her name up, checking for any changes in address or name additions. No changes. Phew.

I also learned you can search for deaths on the Social Security Death Index. Ross was seven years older than Nora. I didn't want anything to happen to him, but I wondered if contacting her would be easier after he passed away.

I raised my eyebrows and typed in his name and birth date. Although there were many Ross Bowers, none fit his age or the address I had for them.

Accepting this information with a crisp nod, my hands paused over the keyboard. What about Nora? I assumed no one in her family would contact me if anything happened to her.

"Okay, Nora Bowers, born July 1, 1929," I said out loud as I typed it in. "Lives in Riverside County. Here we go."

Out of my mouth came the guttural, devastated scream of a wounded animal. The computer showed her death on March 10, 2007. Four and a half months ago.

"She's dead?" Tears, sobs, and moans sent me collapsing to the floor, kicking and flailing my arms.

All this time brooding about her, and she's gone? This is how it ends? I never got to meet her. Everything disappeared in a snap. No family to contact, no birth father's name, nothing. I pulled myself into a fetal position, rocking. This was worse than anything else I'd been through. I sobbed and sobbed. My cries bounced off the walls, carrying my distress through every room.

Looking to heaven, I pleaded, oh please God, help me understand. You brought me this far to tell me no? To slam the door shut, one I can never open again. How can this heal my heart? How can this be the answer?

My mind was numb, and my head pounded. I tried to stand on weak, trembling legs and made it as far as the living room couch. Clutching my stomach, I pressed back the nausea. My vision blurred as I wiped away the streaming tears. I couldn't move or get off the couch. Staring at nothing, I lost track of time. Had it been five minutes, ten minutes, thirty?

I rubbed my hand over my heart. Ouch, it hurt deep inside. I needed to blow my nose and wipe my eyes. The bathroom seemed miles away. Too far to think about.

Hayley had been at a neighbor's house, and when she came home, I was still crying.

"Mom, are we still...what's wrong?" Alarm made her voice squeak, and she rushed over to me. "I've never seen you like this. What happened?"

Looking up with red, raw eyes, I tried to produce a small smile and failed.

I cleared my throat, but it didn't help. No sound came out of my open mouth.

Hayley's eyes widened. "I'll go get you some tissues." She hurried to the bathroom, returning with the entire box.

"Thank you." I wiped my cheeks and dabbed my eyes. I pointed to the computer.

"You want me to see something?" She walked over to the computer and read the data. "Oh, no! This is what you found out today? She's been gone since March of this year, and you never knew. Oh, Mom. I'm so sorry."

She sat beside me on the couch, wrapping her arms around my neck. I leaned into her hug and started crying again. My body shook, and my tears dampened her shirt.

Hayley was weeping, too. Her arms held on tight, willing my body to calm down. I leaned back and looked into her adoring face. My sweet, compassionate daughter. We both reached for tissues at the same time. I blew my nose; Hayley wiped her eyes and dabbed at her wet shoulder.

"I cried all over your shirt," I stammered.

"That's okay. It'll dry." She blew out her breath. "I hate to see you this way. What a shock, Mom. You thought maybe someday you could meet her. I can't imagine how you must feel."

I tried to clear my thoughts. "It's been a rough day. You were about to ask me something."

"It doesn't seem important now. I was asking if we were going to bake chocolate chip cookies today."

"Yes, I have all the ingredients. Let's take the butter out to soften it." I stood and trudged, stiff legged, into the kitchen, standing in front of the open refrigerator door but not moving.

"Butter, Mom," Hayley uttered.

"Right, butter." I took the butter out and placed it on the counter.

"I can make dinner tonight," Hayley offered.

"Thank you. As luck would have it, we're having the rest of the stir-fry chicken. All we need to do is warm it up."

I left the kitchen and went into the bedroom and looked in the mirror. My face was red and blotchy, my hair disheveled. I didn't want to scare Brent and Nate like I had Hayley. It was time to clean up.

I could hear Hayley in the kitchen mixing ingredients for the cookies. The oven beeped, signaling it had reached the temperature. I heard Nate come in through the front door and say hi to Hayley. I could hear them talking in the kitchen.

I sat in my favorite chair, staring out the window. The world continued as if nothing had changed. Our neighbors laughed in their backyard, kids played out in the cul-de-sac, birds flew by. Here I sat, isolated and alone. I didn't want to infect my family with my doldrums. Hayley and Nate were having fun in the kitchen. I covered my face with my hands, swallowing back the tears.

Brent came home at six o'clock. He must have inhaled the smell of warm chocolate chip cookies because I heard him say, "Oh boy, it smells good in here. You guys have been busy."

"I made the cookies. Nate helped eat the cookie dough." I heard Hayley say. "Mom had some bad news today."

"Where is she?" asked Brent.

"I think she's in the bedroom. I haven't seen her since I got home," said Nate.

He found me sitting by the window, staring at nothing. "Rough day?" He walked over to my chair and squatted down.

I looked into his eyes. My own eyes were still puffy and unfocused. My voice trembled. "I was on the computer looking for more info about Nora." I explained what I found in a scratchy, hesitant voice.

He pulled me into his arms. His hug affirmed years of empathy and went all the way through to my heart. I wanted to stay locked in his arms forever. He stepped back and held my hands. More tears gathered in my eyes.

"What a terrible way to find out about her." Brent frowned. "You never expected her to be the first to die. Not at seventy-seven."

I stared down at our joined hands and choked back a sob. "Now everything is gone. This is the end of the end. No one will try to find me. I've lost Nora, Katie, my birth father, the whole connection."

"It's hard to make sense of it right now. You're still numb." He squeezed my hands. "I think we need to find out how she died. Is there any way to get a copy of the death certificate?"

"I'll look it up tomorrow. Tonight's my crying jag. I'm drained. Come into the kitchen and get some dinner."

"Tomorrow's soon enough," he agreed. "I'm hungry and ready to have chocolate chip cookies for dessert."

We sat together around the table. I didn't know if I'd be able to eat anything. My stomach was churning, and my head was still pounding. The kids watched me pick at my food through the whole meal.

"Do you feel any better, Mom?" Hayley asked.

"A little. I can't stop crying." I winced. "It hurts. We could've spent two years getting to know each other. I might have had a relationship with Katie, too." I folded my arms over my chest.

"We wish it would've turned out differently for you. This sucks," said Nate in a loud voice.

"We'll clear the table and do the dishes," Hayley volunteered.

"Thanks. I need quiet, reflective time with God."

They carried the dishes to the kitchen and started the cleanup.

Heading back to the bedroom, I closed the door. Instead of throwing accusations at God, I got down on my knees. I thanked Him for all my blessings and prayed for understanding in this situation. I prayed for Nora's family and their loss, to find healing in my heart, and to let go of hurt and blame. Sniffles accompanied my prayer time. How many tears would I cry before there weren't any left.

I heard the TV and the kids' doors close. We were all in hibernation. Half an hour later, I'd had enough of replaying it all over and over. I left the bedroom and sat on the couch beside Brent. I snuggled close, savoring his warmth. He patted my leg. We sat in compatible silence, watching the news. He seemed to understand my quiet demeanor. Hayley and Nate came in to say goodnight at nine thirty. After an hour, we turned off the TV and lights. My movements were still slow and clumsy. On autopilot, I went through my nighttime routine. Climbing into bed, I sighed. I needed to turn off my mind and sleep. Brent and I cuddled and kissed. Drained, I drifted off.

The next morning, my eyes ached, and my limbs were heavy. Moving at a slow pace, I let the kids sleep in. Brent got up and got ready for work.

"I'm sorry I'm not much help today," I said, blurry eyed.

"It's all right. I'll fix a bowl of cereal for breakfast."

The kids woke up right after Brent left.

"Thanks for letting us sleep in," Nate yawned, rubbing his hand through his hair.

"I'm walking over to Chelsea's today to swim," Hayley added. "Kara and Jasmine are going, too."

"What time? Nate, do you have anything today?"

"Eleven o'clock," Hayley said. "We'll have a snack after swimming, then I'll be home."

"I'm going down to John's later," said Nate.

"Okay, I'm glad you both have fun things to do."

I filled my day with menial tasks. Laundry, vacuuming, dusting. I pushed the vacuum cleaner harder than normal, trying to suck all my negativity into the bag. My foggy brain didn't want to recap yesterday. That was fine with me. When Hayley got home, we went to the grocery store. I let the kids pick out what they wanted for dinner this week. I told them anything was fine, as long as it was easy to cook. We purchased ground hamburger, corn tortillas, avocado, chips, cheese, and salsa for taco Tuesday. Chicken for our favorite garlic chicken recipe, angel hair noodles, broccoli, salad fixings, brownie mix, and fruit for snacks.

Home again, Hayley helped me put the food away, while Nate ate a banana. Minutes later, they disappeared into their rooms. I love tacos, they're easy to make and fun to eat. Mashing the avocados for guacamole, I added salsa and dipped a chip in the mixture. Popping it in my mouth, I savored the creamy texture and delicious flavor.

I set all the food on the counter, allowing each family member to choose whatever they wanted on their plate. My stomach growled. I didn't have much for dinner last night and very little today. We brought our food to the table, and Brent blessed the meal.

"The guacamole is good, Patrish. I love taco Tuesday." Brent crunched on a chip.

"We do, too," Hayley and Nate chimed in at the same time.

We all laughed. The heaviness in my chest released little by little. I wanted to have a normal dinner, no drama. I leaned back in my chair and watched my family enjoy their meal. I took a cleansing breath. Here is where my heart lies.

The dishes were done, and the food was put away. Hayley went to her room to read, and Nate sat with Brent on the couch watching a Padre's game.

I retreated to the bedroom. Praying and praising God through stressful times appeared throughout the Bible. I picked up my copy and read King David's praises in the Psalms. I looked up toward heaven. David had strong faith even while being pursued by enemies. I laid my Bible on the table and went over to the bed, sitting on the edge, preparing my mind to come before God. I thanked Him for my family and their patience with me as I sorted out my feelings.

Once again, I asked for discernment and direction. I'd been focused on Nora for so many years. It baffled me to think she was gone. I prayed for understanding. I would never get the chance to speak to Nora about my feelings. Please help me be okay with this outcome.

To my absolute surprise, I heard two audible words. *Trust Me.*

"What?" I shrieked. It startled me to hear a clear voice speaking to me when no one else was in the room. I knew the voice came from God.

I ran out of the room and plopped down on the couch next to Brent. Nate had retreated to his room.

"I need your undivided attention for a minute," I told him. I grabbed his arm, my eyes blazing. "I heard God say to me *Trust Me.* I'm not crazy. I heard it. God heard my prayers and spoke to my heart to comfort me."

Brent turned off the TV and looked into my eyes. "I know things like this can happen. What do you think it means?"

"Of course, I want to trust Him. I want to believe it means all is not lost. He's working everything out for my good, like He promises in Romans 8:28. 'And we know that in all things God works for the good of those who love Him, who have been called according to His purpose.' Maybe it would have been too devastating for Nora to meet me. I hope it means we'll have eternity together in heaven."

"God always has a Master Plan. I've never heard a voice. Maybe a still, small inner voice. Your eyes are lit up. I think he wanted to reassure you of His love."

"I've never heard it before, either. It has a calming effect, giving me hope and making me feel better. Are we going to Wednesday night service tomorrow?"

"Yes. The message you got tonight reaffirms our need to be there."

"I'm excited to go, but still emotional. I always cry when we sing praise songs. Tomorrow will be hard. I have a lot to reflect on."

A tingling warmth filled my body as I said goodnight to the kids and got ready for bed. What a difference a day makes. I wasn't over the hurt, and I still couldn't see the meaning behind what I went through. One thing was certain, God's peace covered me like a blanket, and I slept well.

I rose early and went for a long walk. August is hot in San Diego. To avoid the heat, I wore a cap and dressed in light clothes. I moved at a quick pace, my muscles stretching, and my arms pumping. Each step pounding out the frustration from two days ago. I took deep breaths as I inhaled the fragrant smell of roses as I passed by our neighbor's home. Further down the block, bacon filled the air. Dogs barked as I went by, and I heard voices of families getting ready for the day.

Arriving home, Hayley and Nate were dressed and eating breakfast. Brent came down the hall as I zipped through the front door.

"You got a good walk in today." He smiled his approval.

"It helped me clear my head. I'm looking forward to church tonight."

"I am, too," said Brent. "I have an eight thirty meeting, so I need to leave soon."

"You look better." Hayley observed as she passed me on the way to her room.

"I feel much better." I said, "Walking is great exercise. Have you guys made your beds?"

They both shook their heads and disappeared into their rooms.

"I'll be home by five thirty tonight," Brent said. "What time is the service?"

"Seven o'clock. I'll have dinner ready when you get home. We'll need to get there a few minutes early, so the kids can get to their classes."

"Sounds like a plan." Brent picked up his briefcase and gave me a loving, soft kiss. I followed him as he went down the hall to the garage.

I stood in the hall between the kids' rooms and asked, "Hey, guys, what are you doing today?"

"I'm going to the mall with Rachael for a couple of hours. She's picking me up at eleven," said Hayley.

I peered into Nate's room. "I'm going to the water park with John and Brian. I'll be leaving at the same time Hayley leaves."

"Okay, we have church tonight. Dinner's at 5:30. You'll have time for a shower when you get home, Nate."

After the kids left, my mind drifted back to Nora. I squeezed my eyes shut, willing away the inevitable tears. My jaw tightened, and I rubbed my hands down my arms. I don't want to slip back into negative thoughts. In my quiet house, I no longer needed to pretend I was okay. I collapsed on the nearest chair, slumped forward, and ran my hands through my hair. How long would this pain hold me captive? God wants me to give it to Him to let it go. Going to church tonight should help.

Time stood still; my mind trapped in the past two years. Pouting, I gave myself a mental kick. I should have been more aggressive pursuing her or at least, maybe found an address for Katie. I'll never fully understand Nora's reaction to me.

Staring out the window, my eyes lacked focus. I felt the warmth of the sun through the glass, soothing my cold skin.

"Enough," I shouted and made my way to the bathroom and scrutinized my reflection in the mirror. Runny mascara, red nose; not a pretty sight. I splashed water on my face and removed the black under my eyes. My hair stuck out in every direction. I fixed my hair, repaired my makeup, and finally looked decent again.

Hayley came home first. I'd managed to curl my hair and plaster a smile on my face.

"How was the mall? I don't see any purchases."

"We just wandered in and out of stores. I didn't need anything. We had burgers and fries for lunch."

Nate came through the door with a beach towel wrapped around his waist. "I'm going straight to the shower," he said.

I went into the kitchen to make garlic chicken for dinner. Melt butter in the pan, add garlic, and take out the chicken. I knew this recipe by heart. Hayley joined me, stirring the butter mixture. Once the chicken went in the oven, we had time before we needed to start cooking the noodles. Hayley set the table, then went to her room.

I heard the shower shut off and Nate shut the door to his room.

Half an hour later, Hayley returned to the kitchen to make the noodles, while I steamed the broccoli.

Brent came home at the same time I took the chicken out of the oven.

"Dinner smells so good. Must be garlic chicken. One of my all-time favorites." Brent inhaled the wonderful aroma of the garlic.

"Your timing is perfect. It's fresh out of the oven. Go put your things down while I dish it up."

Hayley called out to Nate, "Come and get it! We're ready to eat."

Everyone came back into the dining room and sat in their accustomed places. Brent blessed the meal.

"We should leave here by six thirty," I told them between bites of chicken.

"All I have to do is change my clothes," said Brent.

"I'm ready, are you?" Hayley looked over at Nate.

"Yeah, my hair is still wet, but I'm dressed to go."

I had enough time to clean the dishes and put the food away before we climbed into the car. On the ride over, my knees were bouncing, and I clenched and unclenched my hands. I looked in my purse, checking to see if I remembered the tissues. This might be a crying marathon. No doubt in my mind I was meant to be here.

Arriving at church, Hayley and Nate climbed the stairs to their classrooms. Maranatha Chapel is a big church. The outside appearance is different from traditional churches. No steeples, no red brick, or big wooden doors. It's located in a business district. The main sanctuary is flanked on one side by the two-story classrooms, the other side houses the spacious Fellowship Hall. A large patio sits between the two buildings.

We walked through the double glass doors into the sanctuary. The huge, round room had a stage up front with a dove on the back wall. The pews were filling up, and the worship team took the stage. There were several guitarists, a drummer, and a piano player. We found seats about a third of the way from the front.

We remained standing while John led the opening prayer. The worship team began playing. The first few chords of *How Great Thou Art* filled the room. I half smiled at Brent. Oh boy, here comes the waterworks. Singing of God's mercy and greatness even in times of trouble, I lifted my trembling hand and placed it on my heart. My voice came out in a whisper, not my normal loud and joyful. Tears filled my eyes.

Brent stepped closer to me and put his hand on my arm. I looked at him, and our eyes met. I gave him a weak smile.

The song ended, and I pulled a tissue out of my purse and wiped my eyes. I took a deep breath, only to hear the chords of the next song. "For The Lord God Almighty Reigns." My favorite song. The one that always makes me cry whether I'm happy or sad. It was a good thing I had the tissue in my hand already.

I love to sing this song. My body responds with an increased pulse rate, a light sensation, and my hands lifting to heaven. Tonight, I had my head down, eyes closed as the tears poured into my tissue. I'm grateful to God for His love and mercy, but all I could do tonight was weep. It was hard to accept this road He asked me to travel. I needed to accept that a relationship with Nora wasn't in His plans for me.

The next few songs took me deeper into reflection. I looked upward, wanting to connect to God. The church sounded like a choir from heaven. Beautiful, melodious voices sang "My Jesus, My Saviour" and "Here I Am To Worship."

I bent down, picked up another tissue, and caught Brent's eye. His eyebrows drew together, his eyes soft with understanding. The last song, "Shout To The Lord" was easier to sing. I leaned into Brent and took his hand. My voice quivered. I managed to sing most of the song without tears.

The worship team left the stage, and we all sat down. Sometimes at church, you hear a message that seems to have been written for you. Pastor Mark spoke about forgiveness, surrender, and following

God. No turning back, all in. I nodded as he spoke, desiring the willingness to give it all to Him.

At the end of the service, I whispered to Brent, "I'm a mess. Can we get to the car as fast as possible?"

"Okay, the kids know to meet us there."

We hurried out of the church. I kept my head down as we crossed through the patio to the parking lot. Nate and Hayley showed up a few minutes later.

"Uh, Mom, what happened in church? Your face is tear stained." Hayley climbed into the back seat.

"I look like I went to a funeral instead of church, don't I. Worship songs sink into the deepest part of my soul. Tonight the songs were almost more than I could take. I'm glad we came, but it brought up all my tender feelings."

Nate patted my shoulder. "It'll get better, Mom."

When we got home, I knew I needed to fix my face—again. I studied my reflection and thought about Nate's words. May they be true.

It seemed all week there were reminders of God's promises through songs on the radio when I was in the car. I cried hearing Natalie Grant's song "Held" and couldn't back the car out of the driveway. I took comfort in knowing God promises He would be there when everything falls apart.

I attended a women's Bible study and found myself right where God wanted me to be. Our group sat in a circle as we discussed the roles mother's play. Nurturers, confidants, defenders. I told them about my loving adoptive mom and the rejection I got from my birth mother.

"I found Bible verses talking about mothers which help emphasize our roles biblically," our leader Carol told us. "You all have a copy. Let's go around the circle and each read one verse. Pamela, will you go first?"

"'As a mother comforts her child, so I will comfort you, and you will be comforted over Jerusalem.' Isaiah 66, verse 13."

"You're next, Vicki."

"Proverbs 31, verse 25. 'She is clothed with strength and dignity; she can laugh at the days to come.'"

Everyone looked at Sue. "You'll have to skip me this time," she stammered, holding her hand over her eye. "I need to fix my contact lens."

"Okay, Patrish, go ahead."

"All right. 'Can a mother forget the baby at her breast,'" I stammered, my voice shook, and tears pooled in the corner of my eyes. "'And have no compassion on the child she has born? Though she may forget you, I will not forget you. See, I have engraved you on the palms of my hands, your walls are ever before me.' Isaiah 49, verses 15 to 16." Then the deluge of tears.

I looked up to see stunned faces staring at me.

"Of all the verses for you to read, that one hit the mark," said Vicki.

Beth said, "From now on, when I read or hear that verse, I'll think of you."

"How amazing for God to skip Sue, so you could be the one to read that verse," said Sandi.

I wiped my eyes. "It's a beautiful verse and perfect for me. I've read it before, but there's new meaning in it now."

Carol laughed. "I don't think we need to keep going around the circle. We've established God is here, working in our midst and honoring mothers."

CHAPTER SEVENTEEN

It took a few weeks to stop the waves of emotion from turning my mind into mush. One minute I could go about my daily tasks, and the next minute collapsed into a curled-up ball, letting out uncontrollable sobs.

Brent and I agreed on the necessity of getting a copy of Nora's death certificate. Sitting at the computer, I logged into the Recorder, County Assessor for death certificates in Riverside County.

"Okay, Brent, I'm on the site. Looks like they have two types of certificates. An authorized copy or an informational copy."

He looked over my shoulder. "What's the difference between the two?"

"The authorized copy has the official seal, but you need to prove you're a family member, which I can't, but that's the one I want. The other one anyone can get. To obtain either, I need to fill out an application online, then take it to one of the offices. They have one in Temecula."

"That's an easy drive. Friday's a free day for me."

"Okay, it's a plan."

Waiting for Friday to come, I found myself rearranging the kitchen cupboards, checking the clock every ten minutes, and tuning out my family's conversations.

"Mom, hello, are you listening to me?" Nate sighed loudly.

"I'm sorry, Nate. My mind is somewhere else. What did you say?" I turned to look at him.

"I was asking if I could take the car on Saturday. John and I want to go to the beach."

"Let me check the calendar." I drifted over to our family wall calendar. "Looks clear. Make sure you vacuum out the sand when you get home."

"We will." Nate grinned. "Thanks, Mom."

After three very long days, Friday came. I rambled from room to room with no clear destination. My fluttering stomach competed with the pounding of my heart.

Brent finished his breakfast and pulled the car out of the garage. I climbed in, and my hands shook while fastening the seat belt.

Brent's eyebrows furrowed. "Are you okay? You look pale."

I turned toward him and bit my lip. "Yes, and no. I need to find out how she died. What if I find it was from something genetic? Is it better to know or not to know?"

"You'll find out soon enough."

I sat back, deep in thought. The sun reflected off the foothills and pavement. I pushed my sunglasses higher on my nose. I leaned my right elbow on the armrest, put my chin in my hand, and watched the cars pass by. I tapped my foot to the gentle songs on the radio. Brent seemed relaxed as he drove, a small smile on his lips.

We saw the exit signs for Temecula and left the freeway at our designated road. I gave Brent directions to the office, and we parked.

"Moment of truth." I breathed.

Entering the small office, I took my spot behind three people in line, and Brent stood close beside me. Two more people came in and stood behind us.

When the clerk signaled us, I took a deep breath and stepped up to the window.

"I'd like an authorized copy of the death certificate." I slid my application under the window.

The clerk reviewed it and asked, "May I see your identification, please?"

I handed her my driver's license. "Nora Bower is my birth mother," I stammered.

She looked up Nora's name on the computer. "I found her certificate. You can get a copy from this office. It'll be twenty dollars."

After handing her the money, I looked at Brent wide eyed as the clerk left to go in the back.

"Do you think it's an authorized copy?" I asked.

"Hard to tell." He shrugged. "She didn't seem fazed by your name or saying Nora's your birth mother."

The clerk came back and handed me the certificate with the seal. I was officially recognized as Nora's daughter by Riverside County.

We thanked her and went outside.

"Yes!" I pumped my fist in the air. I wanted to read the information, so I slowed my pace and started at the top. It listed her husband's name and the residence where she died.

I stopped walking, and my mouth dropped open. "Brent, she died in a facility in Rancho Mirage, not at home or at a hospital."

I read further down. The top line under cause of death read cardiopulmonary arrest.

"She had a heart attack?" I squeaked out to Brent. "Next it lists acute renal failure and sepsis. What do all these terms mean?"

"I don't know," said Brent.

On the ride home, I studied the document. Her ashes were scattered at sea.

"Renal failure is common when the body shuts down," Brent told me. "Sepsis doesn't sound good."

I covered my face with my hands. "Reading this doesn't help me understand how she died. It makes me sad to think she died at seventy-seven and suffered. It stated she'd been sick for weeks. It must have been the reason for being in a nursing facility. Poor Ross. He's seven years older than her but had to watch her deteriorate and die."

"It is sad. Katie must have been devastated, too."

"This is a lot to process. I don't know what I expected to find. At least it wasn't cancer. I'd still like to know my medical history. I have a little bit from her side, but what about my birth father's side?"

"It's helpful to know all the details. I'd bet more than a few adoptees have no idea what's in their medical history," said Brent.

I reread the death certificate over and over on the ride home. What happened? Did she have a painful, drawn-out death? Or was she unaware of what would happen. Did Ross spend every day by her side? Katie proved to be the only link left. How do I find her? I cringed. Would this family ever accept me?

CHAPTER EIGHTEEN

Nine years had passed since I learned about Nora's death. I never pursued finding Katie. I knew what city she lived in but didn't try to contact her. I used the excuse of not wanting another door slammed in my face. In those years, Hayley got married to Kolton Meyer. Nate moved to Pennsylvania and was getting ready to marry Anna in two months. Brent continued in the financial world. I worked part time helping Brent and spending time with Mom. At a spry eighty-seven, she still lived independently. Those nine years seemed to melt away. We sold our home and bought a two-bedroom condo.

Brent and I cuddled up on the couch. "There's another commercial for Ancestry and taking the DNA test," I said. "I don't know if Nora told the truth about my birth father's nationality. Maybe she never told him about her pregnancy."

"Are you thinking about doing the DNA test?" he asked.

"It would be great to know my true origins. It looks like a simple test. I'm going to order one."

I went to the computer and ordered my test kit online. It came in about a week. Spit into the tube, add chemicals, and off you go. Ancestry told me it would take about four weeks to process. Two weeks later, I got an email with my results.

"Brent, look, my results are on the Ancestry site. Let's see if what Nora told them is true."

He read with me. "It has a lot of details."

"Okay, it says I'm 41 percent Swedish, 39 percent Scottish, 5 percent Irish, 12 percent English and Northwestern European, and 6 percent trace. It says the trace is smaller amounts of combined areas. Here's what Nora told the adoption agency according to the sheet I got. Birth mother: English and German. Okay, a match. Birth father: Swedish, Scottish, Irish. It matches, too. She must have told him about being pregnant and found out his ethnicity."

"Now you know the truth," he said gently.

"I'm fascinated by this site. I'm going to spend more time exploring what all this means."

The site showed a world map with circles around the areas my ancestors came from. It also included little pieces of history for the different regions.

After reading about the regions, I saw an area for DNA matches. I hadn't explored the idea of using it to find family members. Sitting straighter in my chair, I opened that section. There was a notification for a possible match. It listed a female as an extremely strong match for a first or second cousin. She'd left me a message. I leaned closer to the computer to read it.

> Our DNA results from Ancestry state we may be first cousins. My grandparents' last names are Johansson, Hagen, and Donovan. Are any of those familiar to you? My name is Amanda Hagen Cleary. I've been working on my family tree. Your name popping up is a surprise to me. I thought I knew everyone.

I tilted my head to the side and blinked. My hands hovered over the keyboard.

Wow. I'm adopted and took the test looking for my heritage. I found out my birth name is Diana Donovan. Maybe we are related. I didn't know if she gave me his last name or made it up. I welcome finding out all I can about any family members. If you could let me know more, I'd appreciate it, Amanda.

I shouted out to Brent in the other room. "I have a possible family connection. Her name is Amanda and one of her family names is Donovan." My voice hitched. "I'm in shock and excited at the same time. This is more than I hoped for when I took the DNA test. This would connect me to my birth father's family. We're talking right now through email on the site."

Brent came back. "I sure hope this is it. After all this time of waiting, you deserve to know."

Amanda and I continued our email conversation.

I'll see what I can do. How old are you? When and where were you born? Do you have anything else to go on? I hope this turns out to be a family connection for you. I'll work on it from my side.

My birthday is Nov. 5, 1955. I found out my birth father served as a naval officer stationed in Hawaii. My birth mother met him there. I was born in San Diego. He'd been described as five feet ten inches tall, medium husky build, dark blonde hair, blue eyes. His father had blonde hair, blue eyes, and his mother had brown hair, blue eyes. I hope this helps. I'd be excited if this is a connection. Thanks for looking into it.

The return email came immediately. My hands covered my mouth and stifled a gasp.

Okay, Patrish, take a deep breath. I know who your birth

father is. He's my uncle and godfather. His name is Ron Donovan. He's still alive and lives in Washington state. I can't keep this to myself. I'm going to ask his sister, Donna, if she thinks I should call him. You have cousins, aunts, uncles. I hope everyone in the family will be as excited as I am to have found you. I'll get right back to you, cousin!

Leaping in the air, I almost knocked over my chair. I jumped around the room yelling, "I found my birth father. He's still alive. Now I have a cousin, too. Amanda knew right away. This is surreal. One quick click on the keyboard. I have a new family."

I danced around the room with my hands in the air.

"This is fantastic." Brent watched me laughing.

I pulled him over to the computer. "Look, another message."

I spoke to Donna. She said call him! So, I'm calling him right now. Oh, darn. No answer. I'm in Manchester, Connecticut, the same town your birth father, Ron, grew up in. I'm married with two grown, married daughters and four grandchildren. You?

This blows me away. I didn't know if he was still alive or where he lived. I'm married and have a grown son and daughter. Hayley's married, no grandkids, yet. I hope I'm not a big, unhappy surprise for him. What else can you tell me? I'm curious about his life. Thank you so much for reaching out to me.

I'm talking to him on the phone right now. He wants to know your birth mom's name.

I held my breath and answered, **Nora Long.**

He wants to know your name and number. He'll probably need a little time before he calls you.

My forehead creased. A quick question, followed by an answer:

Did he seem surprised or upset?

He seemed surprised. He's a good guy. He'll call you after he stops shaking. Here's his number in Washington.

I stared at the message, my heart racing.

I'm shaking, too. Do you feel comfortable telling me a little about him? Wife, children, other family members?

Let's get off the Ancestry site and exchange personal email addresses so we can talk. I'll send you pictures. He's a widower and has two sons. He served in World War II.

A wide grin spread across my face.

I can't believe we're cousins. Here's my email.

I heard the ping of an incoming email. Opening it, I shrieked. She'd sent a picture of herself holding a sign, Hi Cousin.

I showed it to Brent and tears filled my eyes.

"She accepted me as family right away. This is an answer to prayer. It's been a long wait, but worth it." I stared at the picture. "She's going to send me pictures of the whole family. Do you think we look alike? She's three years older than me. Her hair is white, but she has the Donovan blue eyes."

"Your noses look similar. It's hard to tell. How long has it been since you started the search?"

"You're not going to believe this. Exactly eleven years ago today. February 28, 2005. God asked me to trust Him. I had no idea where this road would take me. I'll never doubt waiting on the Lord. Psalm 27:14 says, 'Wait for the Lord; be strong and take heart and wait for the Lord.' Now I know what it means."

The pinging of new emails brought me running back to the computer.

I hope I didn't give the old guy a heart attack, and he contacts you soon.

A quick answer as I tapped my foot against the chair leg.

Yes, what a shock. I bet he's thinking about what to say to me.

He'll look at it as a positive in his life. You have two half brothers and five other cousins. My mother was Ron's sister. She passed away in 1988. His other sister, Donna, lives in Florida. She's the one I called for advice. His brother Raymond also lives in Florida. I've been actively building our family tree. I'll send you the tree right now, so you can see all our family. I've become the family historian.

The next email had a beautiful, amazing family tree.

I burst into tears. "Brent, I have a family tree." My voice cracked, and my nose ran.

Always a good sport, he came back into the room and read the email.

"She's done a lot of research," he remarked softly, swallowing.

I turned around. Our eyes met, conveying the importance of this finding.

I was excited reading the information to Brent. "Look how far back she's traced the family. Great-great-great-grandparents. It starts with them and goes all the way to Amanda's children and grandchildren. She even has pictures. A lot of Swedish names are there. Irish names, too. I have more questions to ask her. Knowing I'm a part of this family gives me goosebumps."

Okay, now I'm intrigued. Were you close to your grandparents? Did the families get together often? All the cousins are close in age. It would've been fun. Looking

at the tree, I see my half brothers are Blake and Daniel. They each have a son. This is wonderful for me. A
place for me to belong, genetically speaking. I grew up
with two brothers and a sister. Lindsay, Blake, and Josh.
Now, I have two brothers named Blake. You know I'm
going to ask you a million questions. How long have you
and Peter been married?

Phew. I had packed a lot in that paragraph. I hope Amanda is
patient with me. I never expected to have a family tree to explore.

I printed a picture of my tree.

I figured I had asked enough questions for now. I'd spent a lot of
time on the computer. Time to put it on pause. I carried my family
tree into the living room. I couldn't take my eyes off the pictures. I
loved the fact that I had Swedish relatives. My mom is Swedish on
her mother's side. I adored my cute, petite grandmother.

I checked the emails several times during the night. Amanda must
have been exhausted, too. Tomorrow would be soon enough to dig
back in. I took a picture of the photo of the family tree and sent it to
Nate and Hayley in a text message.

It doesn't seem real, they're only names and faces. We
didn't grow up knowing them. It's hard to think of them
as family.

I sat on the bed and texted him back,

It's abstract for you. I've waited my entire life to find all
this out. I love the pictures and the names. I'm excited
to find them, but don't know how they'll feel about me.
We've lived apart, grew up in different states. They don't
know I exist. Let's hope it turns out better than it did with
Nora's side of the family.

I know I can't control their reaction, but I've come a long way
since that terrible rejection. I shook my arms.

Move forward.

Ping. A text from Hayley:

> I like Amanda. From what you've said, she seems nice.

I nodded as I replied,

> Yes. She never questioned being cousins. Plus, she called my birth father right away while we were sending emails. That girl works fast.

I laughed out loud. Energy buzzed through my body. I jumped off the bed, thinking about my new family. Not to replace the one I grew up with, but this was a welcome addition.

Later that night, I sat down on the couch to study the family tree again. Brent sat next to me.

"Two half brothers and five cousins. I hope Amanda's ready for all my questions." I blew air out of the corner of my mouth. "Her mom and dad are Evelyn and Joseph. Her brother is Michael. The other cousins are James, Conner, and Lynn. Looks like one of my cousins, Sam, passed away. Donna's son. They'll all be surprised to hear about me. I wonder when she'll tell them."

Brent scooted over closer to look at the names and faces. "I guess the biggest question is how your half brothers will feel. This is more personal for them since it's their dad."

I gave a mock shiver. "Makes me nervous thinking about that and the phone call from my birth father, Ron. Wonder how long it'll take him to call. What will we talk about? He might be embarrassed and not know what to say. I don't know, either. I'll let him take the lead unless there's a huge lull in the conversation."

Brent leaned in and gave me a loving kiss. "You've had quite a day. You were faithful to wait for God's timing. He knew the right moment and what joy you were going to experience."

I relaxed back on the couch and smiled. "It boggles my mind that it happened eleven years later. To the day. My expectations have changed. I'm more realistic now. I needed to be refined, and you were right. God's timing is always perfect. I'll know more about where to go from here after I talk to Ron on the phone."

I fell asleep with a smile on my face. Who knows what tomorrow may bring.

CHAPTER NINETEEN

I rose early and bounced out of bed, feeling weightless. Every muscle tingled. I didn't want to wake Brent, so I got dressed without making a sound. The computer beckoned me. It was three hours later in Connecticut. Maybe Amanda emailed.

I tiptoed into the office and closed the door. I opened my email and saw one from Amanda.

> I love you're being curious about the family. I'm happy to give you details. Peter and I have been married for forty-two years. We were high school sweethearts. My parents were, too. That's what can happen in a small town. Our daughters, Shannon and Shauna, are a year apart in age. I'm lucky to have been close to our grandparents. Alice appeared as the typical loving grandmother. Her husband, Walter, seemed more reserved.

I scooted the chair closer to the screen, crossing my legs, and swinging my foot. The email continued,

> Yes, we spent holidays together. Birthdays were a great time. Dan and I have the same birthday. Michael's is one day after us. Our cousin, James, has the same birthday as you. Uncle Ron's job required him to travel a lot. He

couldn't join us for most of the celebrations. I'll let him
tell you about it when he calls.

Another family member with my birthday. What are the odds? I
gave a quiet cheer.

There's quite a lot to tell you. Our grandparents, Alfred
and Thora Johannson, came over from Sweden sep-
arately and met in America, where they were married.
They lived in the house where our parents grew up. On
the Donovan side, our great-great-grandfather, Joseph,
came from County Armagh in Ireland. His youngest child,
Patrick, was our great-grandfather. Your head must be
swimming after all this info. The family tree will help you
keep everyone straight. Talk to you soon, cousin.

She got that right. I left the computer and went into the kitchen.
Placing my hand on my heart, I looked toward heaven. Thank you,
God, I whispered.

I received pictures from Amanda over the next few days. Her
daughters, their families, along with a group picture of the cousins
from around 1998. My half brothers were pictured there, too.

I carried the picture of the family tree with me everywhere around
the condo. I kept saying their names out loud, trying to memorize
names, faces, and birthdays.

Brent chuckled on the fifth day of my obsessive behavior. "You're
talking to yourself again. Pretty soon, I'll know all their names, too."

"I guess I am going overboard. It's all so new, and the genealogy
is fascinating."

Brent reached for me. "I couldn't be happier for you. However, it's
as if you're lost in another world. We haven't done anything together
for a while. How about going out to dinner tonight?"

"Oh, Brent, I'm sorry. You're right. I've been so caught up in all
this." I hurried over and hugged him, putting my head on his chest.

I could hear his heartbeat. "You've been an angel, accepting everything, listening to me talk non-stop about the Donovan's. Yes, that's a great idea. Let's go out to eat."

I lifted my head and looked into his eyes.

He grinned. "It's Friday night, let's go early. How about Outback Steakhouse? I could go for a hearty meal."

"I haven't been cooking very many meals this week. I'm sorry, you deserve a good dinner. Let's leave at five."

We drove to the restaurant and held hands walking in. The noisy dinner crowd hadn't arrived yet, and we were seated right away. Brent ordered the filet mignon, cooked medium, a loaded baked potato, and broccoli. I had my favorite Steakhouse salad, ordering the steak well done. We heard the sizzle of steak as it was delivered to the couple at the table across from us. A mom, dad, and two elementary school-age kids sat behind Brent. The noise level began to rise.

Our dinners were as good as we hoped. My steak had enough red to keep it from being tough.

"This is like date night," I said.

"Yeah, it's nice to get your undivided attention." He smirked.

"I am very sorry. There's been a lot of information and feelings to sort through." I twisted my wedding ring. "Waiting for Ron to call and wondering if we'll get along makes me jumpy."

We finished eating, paid our bill, and left. Back home, we decided watching a romantic movie sounded good, so we sorted through our DVDs. We both chose *The Lake House* and settled close together on the couch. The theme of the movie is improbable, but fun. Star-crossed lovers living in different years yet connecting. We both sighed when the movie finished.

"I love movies with happy endings," I said.

"Me, too. This is one of my favorites." He put his hands on my cheeks and turned my head to face him. "I love you. Asking you out thirty-six years ago was the best decision I ever made. Next to marrying you, of course."

I turned my body to face him. Our mouths came together for a tender kiss. His lips were soft and warm. One of his arms circled around my back, the other over my shoulder, and he pulled me close.

We separated and grinned. "Best decision I made was saying yes to both the first date and marrying you."

I got ready for bed, and the cares of the last few days drifted away. I fell asleep with ease.

On Sunday, March 6, after church, we came home to make lunch. I jumped when the phone rang. "It's probably Hayley. She likes to call on Sunday," I said to Brent. I took the bread out for ham sandwiches.

Then I heard the phone computer announce the originating phone number.

I gasped. "It's Ron! Please pick up the other line and get on the call with me. You don't have to say anything, but it'll be easier to remember later if we both hear it. We can sit at the dining room table."

I put the bread down, swallowed hard, and answered, "Hello."

Brent came out of the office holding the other phone.

A gravely, kind voice said, "Hi, is this Patrish? This is Ron Donovan. I'm glad I called when you're at home."

"Hi Ron, I'm very happy you called."

I heard him take a deep breath, and a way he went, plunging right in. "I did know about you. I must admit, I didn't think about your birth after so much time passed. My main concern now is if you had a good upbringing with your family."

"You don't have to worry; I had a great childhood."

He went on to say it had been so long that he didn't have a very clear memory of Nora. They met in Oahu where Nora was living at the time, and Ron was stationed in the Navy.

"We were the Navy, hot dogs, and beer crowd," he said. "She hung out with a more sophisticated group. I couldn't describe her to you, but I remember her as being pretty. We had met a few times before we went out."

I looked over at Brent. His eyes were fastened on me. I gave him a smile and a nod.

"Unfortunately, when I reached out to her, she didn't want to meet me or hear from me. I found out she died in 2007." I fiddled with a pen on the table. "I hope one day I'll find her daughter, Katie."

Ron said, "When Nora told me she'd become pregnant, I asked her what her plans were. She told me she'd go home to California to have you. She didn't say anything about adoption. I figured that was the end of it. She'd made up her mind. I went back out to sea for eight months. In November, I had a few unexpected days off. I found out from a friend of hers she'd gone down to San Diego to have her baby there. She told me what hospital, and I showed up the day you were born."

My head jerked back, and my eyes bulged. Brent met my stare and blinked. Unexpected tears pooled in the corner of my eyes.

He continued. "I wanted to have a chance to speak to her alone, but her parents were there. I asked her to marry me. Her answer came out as an emphatic no. I wanted to do the right thing. She told me the adoption had been arranged. It seemed a shame you'd be left at the hospital when she went home."

In a shaky, halting voice, I told him, "I have documents stating she and her mom went to the adoption agency at about four months into her pregnancy. Her mom turned out to be adopted, too. They decided this would be the best option."

"When I left the hospital, I knew Nora and I wouldn't meet again. As I said, we were mismatched. I spent a lot of time out at sea. Both in the Navy and after I got out. My job required it. Our marriage would have been hard on everyone, including you."

I put my hand over my fluttering heart. "Thank you for telling me all this. You probably haven't thought about any of it for many years. Will you tell me about your family?"

"Amanda told you I was raised in Manchester. After leaving the Navy, I continued to work on ships. It gave me an opportunity to go around the world. I lived the life of a carefree bachelor until the age of thirty-three when I met my wife Deborah. We got married and lived back East for a while. We moved to the state of Washington to have more land and room for the kids to explore. Our boys, Dan and Blake, grew up loving the outdoors. They're both accomplished rowers, skiers, and became involved in search and rescue. What about your family growing up?"

Brent and I had been looking at each other through Ron's description of his family. I jumped at his question and cleared my throat. I told him about my parents, brothers, sister, and where I lived. I reiterated what a great life I had, full of advantages.

Ron pressed on. "Looking back, it's hard to remember all the details with your birth mother. Since I've had a few days to mull it over, I always come back to how your life is now."

"I'm blessed. Brent and I have been married for thirty-two years. We have two children." I told him about Hayley and Nate, where we raised them, and what they're doing now.

His voice sounded energized. "Fantastic! Two more grandchildren. This gets better and better. I always wanted to come back down to San Diego. Now I have a good reason."

We talked on the phone for forty-five minutes. He was forthcoming with information. I could hear the relief in his voice. We hung up with the promise to talk again soon.

"I'm happy the conversation went well." I stretched. "You heard everything he told me. He sounds nice and genuine. I like him. What a relief for both of us. This could have gone either way. I can't believe we were on the phone for such a long time."

Brent stood and rubbed the back of his neck. "You have over fifty years to catch up on and a lot more stories to tell each other. He's had an interesting life."

I followed him into the office where he put his phone back on the charger. "I agree. It must've been hard on his family for him to be gone most of the time. Even Amanda remembered he wasn't home for holiday gatherings."

"I bet Amanda has more stories to tell you, too."

I put my hand on my forehead in mock exhaustion. "I've had enough stories for one day. That was draining. I'll email Amanda, though, and let her know how it went. Next time I talk to him, I'm going to take notes. He gives a lot of details about his life."

I kept the email short. I let her know how great the conversation went and how much I liked him. Soon, I had a reply from her.

> He told me he planned on calling you today. I've been eager to hear how it went. I'm glad you made a good connection. He's a great guy. He'll want to stay in touch and learn more about your family. You're right, he does have a lot of stories to tell. I can help fill in any gaps pertaining to the whole family. This has been a monumental day for you. Relax tonight, absorb all you've learned. I'll always be here for you. We have more to learn about each other.

Ron and I spoke on the phone every week for the next four months. He had stories about his ship days and raising his boys. He and his wife, Deborah, had divorced years ago, but remained friends. She had since passed away.

During our conversations, he stated he'd like to come down to meet me. It was hard for him, though, to travel alone and get around. I received pictures of his activities in the early years. Also pictures of Amanda's wedding, fishing with Amanda's dad Joe, and a family portrait of his parents with their young children.

I showed Brent the family portrait. "Look how cute these kids are. They took the picture before Raymond was born. Here are some of Ron's activities. They look like a fun family."

"Don't discount the family you grew up with. They hold all your memories," said Brent.

"You're right. It's hard to imagine everything being different. Seems weird to come into the Donovan family at this late date. Families have been raised, homes established, lives lived. I'm a stranger." I crossed my arms.

"At least the ones you've talked to so far don't treat you like a stranger. Everyone seems open and accepting."

"Yes, I'm grateful. Now I want to meet as many of them as I can. Amanda says they have annual family reunions in the summer." My eyes lit up, and a mischievous smile appeared. "She wants to tell them about me at the reunion this summer. I'd love to hear what she says! Maybe we can go to one next year."

"They'll be surprised. I bet she won't make it sound like a big deal. She accepted you right away. She might do a drum roll, though," he said, slapping his thighs in a rhythmic drum roll.

I laughed. "You're right again. She's a gem. Now I need to figure out how to meet Ron. We may have to go up to Washington if he can't make it down here. Could be a fun adventure."

I pondered about when we should plan this trip. We'd flown to Pennsylvania in April for Nate and Anna's wedding. Hayley found out in March she was pregnant with triplets. Yes, triplets. Three tiny humans in her little body. It boggled my mind. She'd need all the help she could get when they arrived. We didn't know the exact due date yet. Her current due date had them arriving in December. Triplets usually come early, so maybe October or November. We'll have to see what happens with her first. I had a lot of things to look forward to.

In July, Amanda emailed me,

> I told all the cousins about you this week at the reunion. They were surprised, but no one seemed upset over it. We all know Ron lived the life of a bachelor for a lot of years. Blake and Daniel weren't there. I know Ron will tell them about you. Conner joked you were hiding in the closet waiting to pop out and say surprise. Obviously,

you weren't, but we all laughed. He has a good sense of humor.

My head fell back, and my breath came out in a shaky laugh. Now they all knew. Except the two who might care the most, my half brothers. I'm glad no one seemed upset. Now it seemed imperative to visit Connecticut next summer. I can't wait to meet everyone.

CHAPTER TWENTY

October 3 started out in a typical fashion. I accompanied Hayley to her weekly doctor's appointment. After performing a stress test, the doctor told Hayley one baby seemed distressed. By now, we knew she was having two identical twin girls and a boy. The two girls were scrunched together causing one of them to have a low heartbeat. We were sent upstairs to do another test. Same results. Our next stop turned out to be the prep room.

Hayley bit her lip and looked at the monitor, then over at me. My sweaty hands were clasped together. I gave her a tight smile. They hooked her up to more machines and monitored her for a few hours. We were unprepared for the next question.

"When was the last time you ate today?" the nurse asked.

"Seven a.m.," Hayley answered.

Uh-oh, a surgery question. I met Hayley's wide-eyed glance. We refocused on the nurse.

"We're going to need to deliver the babies today. We don't want anything to go wrong with the little one in distress."

Hayley's hand flew to her mouth. "Today? My husband's not here yet. We were hoping I could carry them longer."

"You won't be going in for a few more hours. Call your husband and let him know."

"I'll go home and pick up Dad. We'll be back as soon as we can," I said, rubbing her arm and managing a big smile.

Once outside the hospital, I ran to my car. Driving home, my mind went into overdrive. This was the big day. I needed to get Brent, drive back to the hospital, and call Kolton's parents. Dancing through the front door, I started to tell Brent the great news. My phone rang.

"Mom, they're taking me in now!" Hayley had both panic and tears in her voice. "Kolton's not here, you're not here. I don't want to be all by myself."

My eyes darted to Brent. "They're taking Hayley in now. I'll give you the details in the car. We have to leave. She's all alone."

To Hayley I said, "Don't panic. I'll call Kolton again and text him. Someone will be there. We're leaving right now."

Brent grabbed his cell phone while my hands flew over the phone pad. Kolton didn't pick up, so I shot off a text.

> They're taking Hayley in right now. You need to hurry and get there!

Brent and I rushed to the car. I kept looking at the clock as Brent drove. Upon arriving at the hospital, we could not be with Hayley. We saw Kolton's parents, Cindy and Lenny, in the waiting room. They told us Kolton had arrived and was with Hayley.

I couldn't sit still, and I kept crossing and uncrossing my legs. Brent stood and paced. Cindy kept looking at her watch. Lenny looked over at Cindy every time she glanced at her watch.

"I hope everyone's doing okay," I said. "Kara's the one who decided today was the day. She was being squashed by Hannah. We never expected this when Hayley and I came in for her doctor's appointment." I chuckled.

"The important thing is we want them to be healthy. They're premature and most likely will be small," said Cindy.

"Amen to that," Brent exclaimed.

Lenny scooted forward in his chair. "Once they're born, the work starts for all of us. It'll take a village to manage three babies at once."

We all smiled and nodded. The door opened, and Kolton came into the room. "They're here, and all three are healthy. They'll go straight to the Neonatal Intensive Care Unit."

He informed us that the three little miracles made their appearance, beginning with Jax at 3:29 p.m. Kara, our stressed-out baby, came second at 3:30, and Hannah arrived at 3:32. The babies were small. Kara only weighed 2.8 pounds. Hannah 3.2 pounds, and Jax 3.10 pounds.

Lenny and Cindy hugged Kolton before he rushed back to Hayley. Tears gathered in my eyes, and we all hugged and congratulated each other.

"We won't be able to see Hayley or the kids for a while," Cindy said, with a big smile on her face. "Do you want to go next door to Tio Leo's for a celebratory dinner?"

"Yes," I replied, my smile matching Cindy's. "We love that restaurant, and boy, do we have a lot to celebrate."

"Three very important reasons." Brent laughed.

We had a wonderful dinner, laughing and toasting to our new grandchildren. After dinner, we returned to the hospital and found Hayley's room. Brent and I went in first.

"How're you doing?" I asked, rubbing her arm. "Kolton told us about the babies. We're all so happy."

"I hurt. The nurse took me down to see the babies in their incubators. They look so tiny and helpless," she uttered in a tearful voice. "They were whisked away immediately after being born. I'll get to hold them later tonight. I saw the birth weights. They might have to stay in the NICU for a month."

Brent tried to calm her. "I know that's hard. The doctor and nurses were looking out for their welfare."

Hayley winced when she moved around in the bed, trying to get comfortable.

I kissed her cheek. "Lenny and Cindy want to come in to see you, too. We won't be able to see the babies today, so we'll go home, but I'm only a phone call away."

"Awesome job, Hayley. Three healthy babies. I don't know how your little body did it." Brent came over and kissed her cheek, too.

We left and said our goodbyes to Lenny and Cindy. They went into Hayley's room.

"What a day," said Brent on the way home.

"One for the record books, a day to celebrate. It'll take Hayley a few days to recover. I wonder if they have to stay in NICU for the full four weeks."

At home, I circled the third on the calendar.

Three babies, all born in the three o'clock range, on the third day of October.

Brent went into the office to check emails. I followed him in, rubbing my hands together in anticipation.

I asked him, "Now might be a good time to go to Washington to see Ron. How about on my birthday? It seems appropriate to meet him on my special day. It sounds like the babies will still be in the NICU, so Hayley won't need help at home yet. What do you think?"

Brent turned around to face me. "I think it's a good idea. I hope Ron's up for it."

"November 5 is on a Saturday this year. We would only need to go up for one night. I'd like to ask Mom to come, too. He asks about her and what she's like. They're only two years apart in age."

"I'll let you make the arrangements; it should be interesting."

"I'll call Mom first and tell her the triplets have arrived. Then I'll see if those dates work for her. This will be fun."

I dialed her number. "Hi, Mom! Hayley's babies are here!"

"What, this early? That's a shock, but a happy shock."

I told her what time each one arrived and their birth weights.

"Oh, they're so tiny. I hope they stay healthy," said Mom. "How's Hayley doing?"

"She's obviously sore from the C-section. The nurses scooped up the babies and rushed them to the NICU, so she's really bummed she didn't get to see or hold them."

"She'll be able to in a few days. I'm so amazed she has triplets. It won't be long before you'll have a full-time job helping her." Mom laughed.

"Yes, between Brent and I, plus Cindy and Lenny, she'll have a lot of help. I have another reason for calling, Mom. Brent and I would like to go to Washington to meet Ron. Do you want to come with us?"

"Are you sure you want me to come the first time you meet him?"

"Yes, I would like you to come, Mom. He asks about you all the time."

"Well, what day are you thinking about going?"

"On my birthday. We'd go up that Saturday, spend one night, and come home."

Mom laughed. "What could be more perfect than to meet him on your birthday. I am curious about him. I would love to come."

"Yeah! I'll call Ron to see if he's available. I want to tell him about the triplets, too. I'll call you back as soon as I know."

I hung up the phone, so happy Mom wanted to go with us.

I yelled to Brent, "She wants to come." I could hear him laughing when he came out of the office.

"This will be quite a spectacular birthday present for you." He grinned. "Are you going to call Ron now?"

"Yep, the moment of truth. I sure hope he agrees."

I hesitated, then I dialed his number.

"Hi, Ron, it's Patrish. I have two reasons for calling you. First, good news. Hayley had her triplets today. Congratulations! You're now a great-grandfather."

"Wow, isn't this early?"

"Yes, it's early. We knew she wouldn't go full term, but today was a surprise for everyone."

I told him their names and birth weights.

"Three small little miracles. That's wonderful news."

I nodded, even though he couldn't see me. I swallowed hard, and I kept my eyes focused on Brent. "I wanted to check with you about us coming up to Washington to meet you. My mom and Brent would come, too. We're thinking of Saturday, November 5, on my birthday."

"Yes, that would be great." He chuckled. "Northern Washington is a long way for you to come. What if we met in Seattle and stay at the same hotel?"

"We'll get a morning flight, so we should be there sometime after lunch."

We agreed on the hotel he suggested and planned to meet in the lobby on the fifth.

"I can't wait to meet you in person, Ron. See you in November."

I clapped and hooted after I got off the phone. "He agreed. We're really doing this. Almost a year of waiting, and now we'll get to see him."

I booked two rooms at the hotel and three seats on the plane, then I called Mom with the details. I told her we would arrange for a taxi to take us to the airport.

"This is a big step. I hope we get along as well in person as we do on the phone."

"It should be fine," said Brent. "He seems like a nice man. But your mom and I will be there if the conversation lags."

I closed my eyes. "I'm meeting my first biological family member." A smile spread across my face. "A new journey has begun."

CHAPTER TWENTY-ONE

Snuggled in my covers in the dark, I stared at the ceiling. I woke up before the alarm rang. Today was my birthday and our flight to Seattle. Adrenaline raced through my body, and I jumped out of bed to shower first, then wake Brent.

I sang softly in the shower, projected images of the day taking over my thoughts.

Hayley's three babies were still in the NICU. They were getting stronger but were not ready to come home yet. I got out of the shower and dressed in my travel clothes. Seattle would be cold, so I chose black jeans, a long-sleeved T-shirt, and a heavy sweater.

I went into the bedroom.

Brent shouted, "Happy birthday, Patrish."

I jumped and laughed. "Thank you. I didn't know you were up yet."

"I'll take a quick shower and get dressed before breakfast."

"Mom's expecting us at six thirty. We should get to the airport an hour before the flight leaves."

The morning went by fast. We loaded the car and were on our way.

We pulled our carry-on bags out of the car and wheeled them to the front door of the condo. I used my key to open the glass door, then we left our bags in the corner of the lobby. We took the elevator to Mom's condo on the third floor and rang her doorbell.

Mom pulled me into a hug. "Happy birthday!"

"Thanks, Mom." I hugged her back.

"I'm ready. Let me make sure all the lights are off."

Mom bustled around from room to room, closing closet doors and turning off the light in her bathroom.

"Okay, we'll call a cab." I pulled out my phone and gave the dispatcher Mom's address.

Mom came back into the living room. "All set."

Brent pulled Mom's bag to the elevator.

In the lobby, we got our suitcases and waited for the taxi.

It was only fifteen minutes to the airport, so we arrived an hour early.

The TSA check through security moved quickly. We checked the departure board for our flight and found our gate.

"Can we find a place to sit? My knee has been bothering me," said Mom.

"Good idea." I found three seats together, and we sat down. I laughed. "Now we can people watch."

We could see planes taking off and landing while the terminal buzzed with conversations, phone videos, and flight departure announcements.

Most of the travelers seemed to be flying alone, but I did notice a couple of groups. The aroma of coffee filled the air, and most everyone was looking at their phones.

"Do you want coffee, Mom? We still have time before boarding."

"No thanks. I had some before we left."

I crossed my ankles under the chair, jiggling my feet. I put my hands over my growling stomach. I had such an anxious stomach this morning I hadn't eaten breakfast.

Brent looked completely relaxed, and Mom fidgeted, rubbing her knee.

The boarding procedure announcement startled me. We waited until they called for the first group to get in line.

We didn't enjoy pulling carry-on bags, but it would be faster in Seattle to bypass baggage claim. There were plenty of open seats on the plane; each row had three seats. Mom chose the aisle, so her left knee wouldn't be cramped.

Brent heaved our suitcases into the upper bin. "I can tell you packed light," he said to Mom.

We settled in our seats and buckled up. The flight would take about three and a half hours. After takeoff, Mom laid her head back and closed her eyes.

I lowered my voice and talked to Brent about our new grandson. "That was quite a scare with Jax the first few days. Pneumothorax is serious. We're so lucky he's okay now."

"His little lungs were susceptible to it, and Hayley said his lung collapsed. What a blessing to have them in the NICU where there's immediate attention for these little babies."

We talked about our new grandchildren most of the flight. After about half an hour, Mom woke up and joined in our discussion. The flight was uneventful, and we had a successful landing.

"Mom, Sea Tac is a big airport. I didn't want you to get tired, so I asked for a wheelchair."

"That's fine with me. I'd love to get a ride." She laughed.

The wheelchair was waiting at the bottom of the jet bridge. Mom settled in, and Brent and I followed the attendant as she whisked Mom away.

"Where should I take you?" she asked, while maneuvering the chair through the crowd.

I told her we needed the shuttle and gave her the name of the hotel.

"I'm glad we can follow someone who knows where they're going. I would've gotten lost," I babbled. I tried to catch my breath while dragging my suitcase behind me. "She really walks fast, and this airport is huge."

Brent was pulling both his and Mom's suitcases. "Your mom couldn't have walked all this way."

The crowded airport had several elevators, escalators, and stairs to access the multiple levels.

"How in the world do people know which direction or elevator to take?" I said. "I'm all turned around."

We followed the attendant to the elevator and got off at the third floor of the parking structure. Mom stood, and we thanked the attendant. We rested on the welcome benches while we waited for the shuttle.

Despite the cool air, my hands were sweaty, and my stomach was restless. I was fifteen minutes away from meeting Ron.

Mom and Brent chatted during what seemed like a long shuttle ride to me. I sat quietly and stared down at my hands. The shuttle pulled into the circular driveway of the hotel. We disembarked and waited for the driver to unload our suitcases.

The rugged lodge interior of the huge hotel lobby was impressive with high vaulted ceilings. We located the check-in counter off to the right and a bar straight ahead.

We got up to the counter, and Brent checked us in while I scanned the lobby, searching for Ron.

"Let's take the suitcases to our rooms, then find Ron," said Brent.

I sighed, not trying to hide my disappointment. "I don't want to go to the room first. I know you're right, but I want to see him."

Brent laughed. "Are you pouting?"

I was for sure.

Brent studied me for a few seconds but didn't budge. "We'll hurry."

Our rooms were on the first floor, so it didn't take long. We put our bags in our rooms, and then met Mom in the hall and went back to the lobby.

Across from the front desk, a gentle fire crackled in a magnificent stone fireplace that stretched from the floor to the ceiling. We walked toward it, and as we got closer, I noticed a walker next to a group of chairs.

We rounded the corner. I gasped and a huge smile spread across my face when I saw Ron.

He rose from his chair and ambled two steps toward me. In the early days, I would have run up to him and given him a big hug, but I had learned to temper my exuberance.

"Ron, at last, we're face-to-face." I hugged his shoulders with one arm, and he hugged my waist.

I introduced Mom and Brent. He shook their hands, directed us to the four comfy chairs, and gestured for us to sit down.

I sat next to Ron, Brent on my left, Mom across from me. His sparkling blue eyes reminded me how strong the genes were in my family.

I looked around the room that was away from the main lobby. "This is a cozy spot."

Ron nodded. "It's more private." His eyes met mine.

He began telling us about his days working on ships and going around the world. His raspy voice was strong as he recounted his many adventures. I had heard these stories during our phone conversations.

Mom and Brent sat back in their chairs, relaxed and listening.

I watched him as he spoke. It was hard to tell at this late stage in our lives if we bore any resemblance to each other. He made small gestures with his hands and leaned forward in his chair, making sure Mom could hear him. I concluded his eyes and the shape of his face were similar to mine.

He spoke without pausing about growing up in Manchester, and later raising his boys, Daniel and Blake, in Washington.

"You've led an active life," said Mom.

He nodded. "I've been able to do a lot of things other people dream about. It did take me away from my family, though." He turned to me. "Tell me about your upbringing, Patrish."

"I love where I grew up. We had three acres and horses. The town was called the Village, and the school was small. The houses were far apart, which meant our parents usually had to drive us to our friends' houses. It was too far to walk, but I lucked out. My best friend lived just down the street." I smiled, remembering the early years.

Ron looked over at Mom. "I doubt Patrish caused trouble. Any stories you can tell me about her?"

Mom laughed. "You're right, she didn't get into trouble. She wanted everyone to get along, and that's not an easy task with three other siblings."

"Blake and Josh loved to roughhouse," I said. "I take that back. I don't think Josh liked it as much as Blake. They're only sixteen months apart, so it caused rivalry."

"I didn't know about most of their antics until years later." Mom frowned. "I guess that's a good thing because thinking about it scares me."

"My sons are three years apart in age. They loved outdoor activities," said Ron and told us more about his life.

I glanced at Mom as she stifled a yawn and noticed Brent's eyes were drooping.

"I think Mom and Brent are ready for a nap. We're not accustomed to getting up at five a.m."

"I am tired," said Brent and shifted in his chair. "A nap sounds good. What about you, Linnea? Do you want to go back to your room?"

"Yes, I admit I'm tired," said Mom. "Are you two staying here to talk?"

"If Ron still has the energy to stay, I'm staying, too. I don't want anything to cut into our time together." I looked at Ron, and he nodded.

"After your nap, we'll go for an early dinner."

"I'll come back when I wake up," said Brent. The three of us stood. I gave them each a hug and sat back down.

Ron's eyes sparkled. "Tell me more about those precious triplets."

"Your new great-grandchildren are wonderful. They're still in the NICU, and we had a scare with Jax's lungs, but he's okay now. It was hard for Hayley to go home without her babies, but she visits them every day and can hold each one. We were able to hold them, too. The important thing is that they are gaining weight and growing."

His entire face lit up. "I can't believe I'm a great-grandpa. Give Hayley and Kolton a hug for me and a kiss for each baby."

"I will. It's going to be a circus when they all come home. I can't imagine the routine we'll have to go through for each feeding and diaper change. We call it 'all hands-on deck.' It will take all six adults to run this show. All four grandparents will have an active part."

Since we arrived at the hotel, we had talked for four hours. I stifled a yawn and rubbed my hands over my face. Our conversation halted as we both stared into the fire. The warmth of the dancing flames was hypnotic. We sat in compatible silence for a few minutes.

I glanced at my watch.

"It's four forty-five. Are you ready to eat? Mom and Brent got less than an hour's nap, but I hope it was enough that they'll feel refreshed."

"Yes, dinner sounds good. I'll go up to my room and get ready, then meet you back here."

I hadn't moved in hours, and I felt it when I stood and stretched my stiff legs. The walk to our room revived me. Brent was still sleeping peacefully.

I nudged him awake.

He mumbled, "Time to get up already? Guess I really zonked out. Five o'clock in the morning is too early to get up."

We both yawned. He got out of bed and stretched his back.

"I need to splash water on my face and brush my teeth," he said.

"Okay, while you're doing that, I'll go wake Mom. We're meeting Ron in the lobby for dinner."

I knocked on Mom's door and called her name. If she was still sound asleep, I wasn't sure she would hear me.

After a few minutes, she opened the door.

"I'm up. I just need to change my clothes," she said.

"I'll go get Brent and be back in a few minutes."

Brent had changed his clothes and was ready to go. I combed my hair and brushed my teeth. I looked in the mirror and mumbled, "I look like a zombie."

Not much time to do anything about that, so I changed out of my rumpled clothes.

"All right, I'm all set. Let's go get Mom."

Mom answered the door on the first knock. She picked up her purse and stepped out into the hall.

Brent's stomach growled. "I'm ready to eat."

I led the merry trio down the hall. "We're meeting Ron by the fireplace. The restaurant is over there, too."

Ron had changed clothes for dinner, and when he saw us, he signaled for us to take the lead to the restaurant.

"Looks like we beat the crowd. Four for dinner," Brent told the maître d'.

"How about a window seat?" he asked, gesturing toward a table with a view of the back patio.

"That sounds great," said Brent.

I sat next to Ron, the window at our backs, with Brent and Mom across from us. The server brought our menus and four glasses of water.

The waiter came around. "My name is Mark. I'll be serving you this evening. What can I get for you?"

Mom and I decided on the chef salad. Brent ordered a hamburger with fries, and Ron wanted the minestrone soup.

Brent said, "We're here to celebrate Patrish and Ron's birthdays." He lifted his water glass. "Happy birthday to both of you. What a great way to celebrate, having you meet for the first time."

We clinked our glasses together.

"This is a special birthday for me," I said. "We missed a lot of birthdays together, but here we are. A toast to Ron and his open acceptance of me."

Ron blushed. "It's special for me, too, getting to meet all of you. I don't travel very much anymore, so thank you for flying up here. I don't know if I could've made it to San Diego."

Both mine and Mom's eyes brimmed with tears.

Ron looked directly at Mom. "I also want to thank Linnea for raising Patrish to become the woman she is today."

"I second that," Brent chimed in.

Mom reached for her purse and pulled out a tissue. "Thank you for the compliment. I'm the lucky one. Patrish and I have remained close, and I cherish my time with her. Thank you for including me on this trip. It's fun getting to know you and hearing your stories, Ron."

Our food arrived. We continued to visit while we enjoyed our meal. When we finished, Ron insisted on paying the bill.

We left the restaurant. "Mom, will you take a picture of Ron and me?"

Ron and I sat together on a nearby bench and smiled at the camera. This was a night I never wanted to forget.

After the picture, we went to the same chairs by the fireplace where we had been sitting earlier.

Everyone stared silently into the crackling fire. We seemed to have run out of things to say.

Brent scrutinized me. "You look tired, Patrish. We should turn in early. You must be tired, too, Ron. Let's meet down here in the morning for breakfast, say, eight o'clock?"

"Sounds good to me."

"We need to be at the airport by twelve, so that should give us plenty of time," said Brent.

"Great plan, Brent." I stood. "Thank you for the great evening, Ron, and for dinner."

"It has been a wonderful time, Patrish."

I smiled. "See you at breakfast."

We left Ron at the elevator. "Thanks again, Ron," said Brent, and we went to our rooms.

I gave Mom a warm embrace and kissed her on the cheek. "Goodnight, Mom. I hope you sleep well."

Brent hugged her, too. "Goodnight, Linnea. We're so happy you came with us."

In our room, Brent asked, "What did you guys talk about while your mom and I napped?"

I put my purse on the chair. "He told me more work stories. I still don't know very much about his sons and what they're doing. I'm assuming he's told them. We didn't get into that part of our relationship."

"Maybe someday you'll meet them, too." Brent turned the TV on. "I hope you don't mind if I watch for a little while. The nap gave me a second wind. I'll keep it low."

"It's fine." I got ready for bed and curled into the covers.

My thoughts were jumbled, and I replayed the conversations of the evening. I still had questions. How did Ron feel about us, what did his sons say when he told them, would Brent and I be able to go to a Donovan reunion? Would I ever see Ron again after this weekend? Stop. Go to sleep. You still have tomorrow with him. At long last, I fell asleep.

The next morning, I knocked on Mom's door at seven forty-five. She was dressed and ready to go. We saw Ron waiting for us by the stone fireplace. Breakfast was being served in the same restaurant where we had dinner. We were shown to a table, and the hostess distributed menus.

Ron pulled out his chair. "How did everyone sleep?"

"I slept fine once my mind shut down." I laughed. "How did you sleep, Ron?"

"It was a long day for me. I fell asleep without any problem."

Brent slid his chair out. "I turned on the TV to unwind."

"No problem for me, either." Mom looked at her menu. "I see what I want. The two scrambled eggs combo plate, with toast, bacon, and orange juice."

I set my menu down. "I'm a light breakfast eater. I'll have an English muffin and jam."

"I'm going to have the French toast," said Brent.

Ron glanced at his menu. "I eat light at breakfast, too. I want yogurt and fruit."

We ordered our food, and Mom and Brent asked for black coffee. The room filled quickly. The noise level rose with clanking dishes and multiple conversations. The aroma of coffee wafted through the air.

Our waiter brought our food. Brent poured a generous amount of syrup on his French toast.

Mom sipped her coffee. "This looks good."

I spread raspberry jam on my English muffin. It crunched as I bit into it. Mom took a bite of bacon. Once again, we had a compatible silence while we ate.

When our plates were cleared, Mom and Brent continued to sip their coffee.

I turned toward Ron. "What's your schedule this morning?"

"I'm waiting for a call from my good friend, Bill. He offered to drive me back up north." His phone rang. "Here he is."

We listened as Ron explained to Bill that he still needed to check out. A few *okays* later, he hung up.

"He's almost here. We should get moving."

Brent paid for the breakfast, and we all returned to our rooms. I checked the bathroom and closet. We didn't want to leave anything behind. We wheeled our suitcases out into the hall. Brent went next door to help Mom with her luggage.

It wasn't necessary for Mom to stand in line, too. She opted to sit in the chairs by the fireplace.

There was a small line at the front desk. Ron was already at the front of the line. A tall gentleman held the handle of Ron's suitcase.

I nudged Brent and pointed to Ron. "That must be Bill."

Ron finished checking out before we got to the front of the line. He walked over to where we stood and introduced Bill.

"I'm all set," Ron announced. "Bill's car is parked out front. Thank you all for a very pleasant visit. I hope we can get together again sometime."

He shook our hands and turned to leave. My face scrunched up, and my smile quickly became a frown. That was it? I turned my questioning eyes to Brent. He was frowning, too. We watched them leave.

"Sheesh, that felt abrupt. Mom didn't get to say goodbye. She's not going to be happy about it," I said, clenching my jaw.

"I'm surprised, too. Maybe Bill was in a hurry."

Ron glanced back at us just before he walked out the door, and my heart suddenly felt sad.

We got to the front of the line, checked out, and went to get Mom.

I explained to her that Ron had already left.

Her brows rose. "What? I didn't get to see him again. We don't know if I ever will."

"We didn't know he would leave so soon. I wanted to bring him over to you. It's too late now. They're gone." I looked down at my feet.

"Let's go out and wait for the shuttle. The desk clerk told me it would be leaving soon," said Brent.

We took our suitcases out front to the shuttle. There were several passengers already seated. The driver loaded our suitcases, we got on board, and the shuttle departed.

I said to Mom, "There will be a wheelchair waiting for us again at the shuttle drop off. I'm still confused by the airport. We need an expert to get us to the right departure gate."

She smiled. "I like going for a ride. It beats walking for a mile."

Brent and I nodded in agreement.

The wheelchair attendant navigated us briskly through the airport.

We got through the TSA checkpoint and to our gate with an hour to spare.

I looked around at all the people traveling here and there. Seated next to Brent, I asked him, "Do you think we can go to the reunion in Connecticut next summer?" My eyes pleaded with him to say yes.

"We'll plan on it. We can go to see Nate and Anna, too. Our newest grandson will be born by then."

I clapped my hands. Something fun to look forward to. I made plans to call Amanda when we got home. She would be eager to know about our visit with Ron, and I could let her know we were coming to Manchester in July.

My mind once again replayed the weekend. Meeting Ron had fulfilled a longtime desire. Maybe if we see him at the reunion in Manchester, I might even get to meet Blake and Daniel. Maybe not.

God's plan has always been at work. My job was to listen and obey.

CHAPTER TWENTY-TWO

February 7, 2017, turned out to be a joyous day for our family. Nate and Anna had a baby boy they named Alex. It was hard being far away from them. There would be many restless, sleepless nights for the new parents. I wished Brent and I could help them, and I couldn't wait to hold Alex. We asked them to send us pictures as he grew. We laughed at his gorgeous head of hair. They had moved out of an apartment and purchased a home. Nate wanted to fix it up and paint Alex's room.

Our next adventure came in July. Amanda said the next Donovan reunion would be July 22. We made plans to spend a few days with Nate and Anna, then drive from Altoona to Manchester. The last time we saw Nate and Anna was at their wedding in April 2016.

We packed our suitcases the night before our flight. "Are you ready for this?"

My eyes lit up. "I've waited a lifetime to see my biological family. I met Ron. Now it's time to meet the rest of the Donovan crew. I want to take a lot of pictures, so I'm glad we got a new camera for the occasion."

"It will be fun to spend time with Nate and Anna, and to see Alex; he's growing so fast. I'm looking forward to seeing their home, too. Even though it will be a brief visit."

Our plane left at seven thirty on Wednesday, the nineteenth. Summer travel was in full swing at the crowded airport. I looked at my watch every few minutes, waiting to get on the plane.

"Getting anxious?"

"Yes, I just want to be there already. We still have a long day ahead, and a stopover in Chicago."

Brent laughed. "You're right, we have a long way to go."

At last, our plane arrived at the gate, and we boarded. The flight turned out to be uneventful. The forty-five-minute stopover in Chicago gave us enough time to eat lunch.

Brent watched me push my salad around the bowl. "You're picking at your food."

"I'm not very hungry, and I have a headache. The cabin pressure on the plane got to me."

"Try to eat a little more," he coaxed. "You'll be hungry later."

I nodded. I wouldn't get a chance to eat once we arrived in Altoona, so I ate a few more bites.

The next leg of our flight passed quickly. We landed at the small Penn State College airport. We picked up our luggage and went outside where Nate waited for us.

I threw my arms around him, hanging on tight. "It's so good to see you again. We can't wait to spend time with your precious family."

He hugged me back in a warm embrace.

Brent pulled him into a bear hug. "Thanks for picking us up."

We put our bags in the back of his car and made the hour trip to our hotel. Nate had taken a few days off work to spend time with us.

We made plans for the next day.

"Is there anything you guys want to see or do while you're here?" Nate asked as he drove.

"I want to spend as much time with Alex as I can. You, too, of course"—I laughed—"and Anna when she's not at work."

"You can spend all the time with Alex that you want, Mom."

"He's probably used to being on a schedule, right?"

"Yes, but it's fine."

"We can just hang out at your house. We don't have to do anything special," said Brent.

"Maybe we could take Alex for walks in the stroller," I said. "And we want to treat you both to dinner and go shopping for things Alex might need."

"Typical mom stuff," Brent joked.

Nate pulled into the circular entrance in front of the Altoona Grand Hotel. "What time should I pick you up?"

"We'll be a little jet lagged. How about nine o'clock? Gives us time to adjust and get breakfast," said Brent.

We got out of the car, and Nate unloaded our suitcases. We hugged him again and went inside to check in. We'd stayed at the same hotel when we came for their wedding. We got our key cards from the front desk and went to our room.

Brent opened a dresser drawer. "Should we put our clothes in the drawers, so they're not too wrinkled?"

I nodded. "You're right, it will help keep them fresh. I'm just so tired."

Brent claimed the drawers on the right and began filling them with clothes. I took the ones on the left and hung a few things in the closet. We turned on the TV to relax. It wasn't too long before sleep overtook me. Traveling across the country is exhausting.

CHAPTER TWENTY-THREE

We ate breakfast at the restaurant and went outside to wait for Nate. Puffy white clouds sailed above us, playing peek-a-boo with the sun, adding to the mild temperature.

When Nate pulled up, Brent climbed into the front seat. I peered through the window and waved at Alex, then climbed in the back and cozied up next to him.

"Hello there, little fellow. We're your grandparents from San Diego, and you are such a cute boy," I told him. "You don't know us, but you will."

His big blue eyes stared into mine. I touched his head, not much hair yet. He gave me a slight smile.

Brent turned around. "What happened to all that black hair he had a few months ago?"

Nate shrugged. "Who knows? It didn't last very long. Now we wonder what color it will be. Probably some shade of blonde, since both Anna and I had light hair as kids."

I lightly rubbed little Alex's head. "I wonder if he'll have curly hair like Anna. Hayley's hair was curly, too."

"It's time for his nap, so we'll go back to the house. He usually sleeps for about an hour and a half. Then you can give him a bottle if you want, Mom."

"I would love that, if he'll let me."

"He'll let you. He's not very fussy as long as he gets fed."

We arrived at their home a few minutes later. Nate picked up Alex in his carrier and took him inside.

I looked around the front sunroom. "I love your house. This is a great playroom for Alex with all the sunlight."

"The downstairs space is perfect for us." Nate took us on a tour. The kitchen was huge.

"I've never had a kitchen this big. Anna loves to cook, so this is a wonderful use of space."

Nate put Alex in his bed next to the couch. He fidgeted, so we spoke in whispers, and a few minutes later, he fell asleep.

Nate started up the stairs. "Let's go up here first. The bathroom is here on the right, Alex's room is across the hall, and our room is here."

I took a quick glance into Alex's room.

"We figured he'd need a crib this month. We're working on getting his room ready, nothing too elaborate. A crib, mobile, and maybe paint some cute figures on the wall."

We went back down to the main floor, and he opened the door to the basement.

"There's a lot of room down here." He pointed to the right. "Laundry room," and then to the empty room next to it. "We want to make this a usable space."

"It is a big room. You can do great things with this," said Brent.

We went back upstairs and sat on the couch in the living room. I couldn't help myself. I kept going over to the bassinet and peeking at Alex.

"He's almost too big for this bed. He's long and slender. You're right, he'll need a crib soon."

"We want to go shopping with you and Anna. You can pick out things you'll need for his room. It'll be fun to shop for accessories," said Brent.

I gave Nate a hug. "He's such a sweet little boy."

He turned to Brent. "Thanks, Dad, that will help. It's amazing how fast expenses pile up when you have kids. Diapers alone cost a fortune."

"We remember." I laughed.

Nate shook his head. "I can't begin to imagine having three kids Alex's age. The number of diapers and bottles Hayley uses must be staggering."

I nodded. "It takes a village, and we all help. Kolton's parents, too. It's fun to have one-on-one time, too, like you get with Alex."

Alex woke up at ten thirty. I put him on my lap and fed him his bottle. Perfectly content, he stared up at me.

"I wonder what color his eyes will be. Maybe he'll have bluish green eyes like yours, Nate."

"I'd love that. Green eyes are unusual, though, aren't they? What color are the triplets' eyes?"

"So far, Hannah and Kara's are blue. We hope they stay that color. Jax has greenish brown eyes. It's fascinating how genetics comes into play."

"I have greenish brown eyes, too," Brent added. "Blue does run on my dad's side of the family. Mom's side is mostly blue."

Alex was watching me, and I gazed at him. "Looks like this bottle is almost gone."

After Alex finished, Nate changed him, and we went across the street for a stroll in the park.

I pushed his stroller. "This is a nice grassy area to have close to your house. He'll have fun playing out here when he gets older."

Nate laughed. "That's one of the reasons we chose this house. Grass we can play on, but we don't have to take care of it."

We made several laps around the park, enjoying the sunshine and talking about Nate's and Anna's jobs.

"Anna will be home at about four thirty. She cleared her schedule so there wouldn't be any late clients today."

"Helping people all day would be tiring. I admire her. Is she enjoying her counseling job?"

"Yes, for the most part. She comes home tired, but Alex sleeps through the night now and that helps."

When we got back to the house, Nate took our sub sandwich orders and left to pick them up. We put Alex on a blanket on the living room floor. He loved playing with his soft toys and putting everything in his mouth. We set up his musical activity mat and put him on his back, so he could reach the hanging toys.

When Nate came back, we sat on the floor next to Alex and ate our sandwiches. By twelve forty-five, he was ready for another nap.

"Eat, sleep, and change diapers; life with a baby," I said.

"How true. On weekends, our schedule revolves around him. He's in daycare during the week."

Later, when Anna came home, Alex was laughing while I made blowing noises.

"Hi, everyone. I see you've found out how to make our little guy giggle. He loves funny noises."

"Hi, Anna. I love playing with him. He has such a fun laugh."

Alex turned toward his mom and reached out to her.

Brent gave Anna a hug. "We couldn't wait to see all of you. Patrish doesn't want to put Alex down."

"He wants his mom now. I guess I'll have to let him go." I handed him to Anna, and Alex smiled at her.

"Can we take you out for Italian tonight?" asked Brent.

"Sounds good. I'm going to change my clothes and Alex's diaper," said Anna.

They came back down a few minutes later. Nate put Alex in his carrier, and we headed for the car. We decided on the Olive Garden, a short drive away.

The wonderful aroma of marinara sauce, fresh baked bread, and melted cheese greeted us as we entered.

"I love Italian food. Could have something to do with my Italian roots." Brent licked his lips.

We were seated at a table for five and placed Alex in his carrier in the extra chair between Nate and Anna.

I ordered lasagna, Nate chose raviolis, Anna spaghetti, and Brent fettuccine Alfredo.

Nate looked across the table at me. "I see Dad still orders the same dinner every time."

I smiled. "Yep, we'd be shocked if he didn't."

Brent raised his eyebrows. "Hey, I order other things. Sometimes I get fettuccine with shrimp."

Nate laughed. "Big change, Dad."

Our server brought salad and breadsticks. The restaurant was filling up. Bussers worked quickly clearing dishes and placing silverware for the next round of patrons.

Our sizzling dinner arrived before we finished our salads. Alex cooed, and we chatted while we ate. The serving sizes were large. All four of us asked for take home boxes.

Back at their house, we put on a movie, taking turns cuddling with our little grandbaby. His eyes grew heavy, so Nate carried the bassinet upstairs, and Anna put him down for the night.

After the movie, we said goodbye to Anna, and Nate took us back to our hotel.

"Today was fun. I miss our sweet family. We don't get to see all the fun stages Alex is going through." I sighed.

"We still have all day tomorrow. We'll take lots of pictures. Let's get some sleep, now."

I closed my eyes. Visions of my four grandchildren playing together filled my mind.

Someday.

CHAPTER TWENTY-FOUR

W e were awakened Thursday morning to the loud, deafening ring of the fire alarm. We scrambled out of bed blurry eyed but wide awake.

"What in the world?" I yelled at the same time scanning our hotel room.

"If this is an actual fire, we have a lot to pack up or risk losing it all," Brent shouted, running his hand through his hair. He checked the door. "There's no heat. I don't see any smoke."

My heart raced. Everything in the room could be replaced, but it would put a damper on our trip.

Someone knocked on the door.

A muffled voice said, "It's safe to open the door."

Brent inched it open. One of the desk clerks stood on the other side.

"Everything is okay. There was a small fire in the kitchen. It has been extinguished. The rooms are safe, as is the rest of the hotel. We're sorry for the scare."

"Thank you for letting us know. We're glad it wasn't serious." Brent closed the door and turned to me, blowing out a huge breath. The fire alarm shut off. Silence.

"What a way to start the morning. I panicked, thinking of how quick we'd have to pack."

Brent laughed. His voice was still shaky. "I was searching for an escape route. Now we know why they post them on the back of hotel room doors."

"Now that we know it's safe, let's get ready for the day. We should skip eating breakfast in the restaurant, though. It might be chaotic."

Brent leaned against the wall. "Good point. I'll get coffee in the lobby and check out the continental breakfast tray we saw yesterday."

An hour later, we climbed into Nate's car and told him about the fire scare.

"Yikes, what a way to wake up. I'm glad it turned out okay."

"We are, too." I climbed into the back seat next to Alex.

"Today, I'm going to show you around Altoona. We'll go by my work, Anna's work, show you our favorite restaurants, and the house where Anna grew up."

The landscape was green and beautiful. Nate told us most of the houses were about seventy years old. We made a big loop, passing the shopping center we'd come back to when Anna got home.

I patted Alex's leg. He was content chewing on his teething ring.

"Thank you for showing us around. We saw some of it when we came out for your wedding last April. I like the rural parts. Long, winding roads, huge green grassy lawns. It's pretty here, but I wouldn't be able to take the winters and all the snow. How can you tolerate it? You're a San Diego boy."

"I like the changes in seasons. I'm always ready for spring to thaw everything out, though. Winters can be challenging and brutal."

"I'd never get Mom to move where there's snow." Brent laughed, turning in his seat to look back at me.

"Nope. I've never lived in it, only visited areas for skiing. I admit, I'm a sunny day girl. I don't like to be cold."

I bent over Alex. "This little guy looks like he's getting sleepy. Should we keep driving around, or take him home to his bed?"

"Better to have him sleep in his comfortable bed. Besides, if he falls asleep in the car, he'll probably wake up when we move him to his bed. We'll head home."

I chuckled. "That's how you and Hayley were as babies. As soon as the car stopped, you woke up. Sometimes, we couldn't get you back to sleep when we put you in your own bed. The catnap took the edge off, and you were ready to play again."

We arrived home and got Alex settled in his bassinet.

"Are you hungry?" Nate asked, going into the kitchen. "We could warm up the leftovers from last night."

"Sounds perfect." I helped Nate, and we brought the food to the dining room table.

"It's amazing how good Italian food tastes the next day," Brent said, popping a fork filled with steaming fettuccine into his mouth.

"I agree. I'm enjoying my lasagna, too."

After lunch, Brent and Nate caught up on all the latest football and baseball stats. I fiddled with my phone.

Alex woke up two hours later. We fed him and got him ready to go shopping. I took him into the front sunroom and laid him on his back.

We heard Anna's car drive up. I lifted Alex from the floor. His little arms and legs flailed as Anna came through the front door.

"Hey there, how's my boy?" she cooed. "Let me put my things down before I hold you."

She set her purse and files on the end of the couch, and I handed Alex to her.

"What a greeting. He got excited when he heard you outside the door. He's a wiggly little fellow."

"I'll take him upstairs while I change my clothes. Are we going shopping?"

"Yes, we want to get some things for Alex's room," said Brent.

We were out the door fifteen minutes later.

"Wait," I said, holding up my camera. "Let me get a picture of the three of you standing in front of your door." They stepped in close together. I took Alex out of his carrier and handed him to Anna.

"Say cheese," I chimed, snapping a cute picture.

The car was a little more crowded with five of us. Brent and I sat on either side of Alex's car seat. He stared at Brent, waving his hands.

"Alex is excited to go." I chuckled. "He must know we're getting things for his room."

We pulled into the parking lot, slid out, and Nate picked up Alex's carrier.

"What theme are you going with for his room?" I asked Anna.

"Primary colors with an animal theme."

When we entered the store, I looked around. "Where do we start? This place is huge."

"Let's start in the bedding department. The comforter and sheets will help us decide on the rest of the decorations." Nate pointed toward the back of the store.

We had fun looking at all the cute designs. We found a jungle theme pattern with lions, tigers, birds, and monkeys. There were sheets and a mobile to match the comforter.

I held up the comforter. "His room is going to look like a zoo. I'll bet he'll grow up loving animals."

"He's already fascinated with our cats. He watches them prowl around the house and play together," said Nate.

Brent pointed to the pattern on the sheets. "Most kids love to go to the zoo. He'll already know all the names of these animals before he gets there."

Anna smiled. "It'll be fun setting up his room. We're ready to move him from our room and the bassinet to a crib. He already sleeps well during the night, and a crib will give him more space."

Nate nodded. "These few items will get the room started. Thank you for buying them for us. The crib should arrive soon." He looked at Anna. "What are we having for dinner tonight?"

"Baked chicken, Greek style potatoes, and salad." She grinned.

"I can't believe it's our last night here," I said. "I wish we could have stayed longer."

"Me, too," said Anna. "But it's been fun, and thank you for the things you bought for Alex."

"You're welcome," said Brent.

"Are you looking forward to the reunion, Mom?" asked Nate.

"All those Donovans in one place should be interesting. I hope I fit in."

"Amanda welcomed you right away. She sounds like she's really nice." Nate noted as we walked to the car. "But I can see why you would be nervous. You were a surprise to them."

Brent climbed into the back seat after Anna snapped Alex's carrier into the holder in the middle. I squeezed into the other side.

"Secrets have a way of getting out. They're like time bombs. Eventually, they explode," I said.

Nate parked at their house, and I got out of the car. "I want to get more pictures of Alex. Treasures to take back home with me."

Anna and I went into the kitchen to prepare dinner. While the chicken and potatoes baked in the oven, I played with Alex and took pictures.

"He has the best smile, like he's posing for the camera. I can't wait to frame these pictures."

The buzzer rang to signal the chicken was done. Anna jumped up and went back into the kitchen. "Alex is photogenic. Makes it fun to take his picture," she called over her shoulder.

I followed her in, taking the potatoes, then the chicken out of the oven. Anna mixed chopped onions, cucumbers, green bell peppers, olives, small tomatoes, and feta cheese in a large bowl to make the Greek salad. She broke up romaine lettuce, added the vegetables, and tossed the mixture with her homemade dressing of olive oil, red wine vinegar, Dijon mustard, and garlic.

"Okay, dinner's ready," said Anna.

Nate and Brent picked up their plates and dished up their food. Anna put Alex in his carrier and set him on the corner of the table.

"This dinner is delicious," Brent said between bites. "Patrish, you need to get the recipe for the potatoes and salad from her."

Anna beamed. "Remind me after we eat, and I'll write it down for you."

"Now you see why I'm not a skinny one hundred and thirty-eight pounds anymore," said Nate. "Anna's cooking is amazing."

I set my fork down. "Well, you look better with some meat on your bones. Thank you, Anna, for helping him get healthy."

"My pleasure. I'm glad he likes my cooking."

We finished eating, and Nate did the dishes while Anna put away the food.

"May I give Alex his last bottle?" I asked.

"Yes, let me warm it up for you."

I sat with Alex in my arms, holding his bottle for him. "I'm going to miss this little guy. He's growing fast. I won't see when he crawls or takes his first step. Make sure you send me lots of pictures."

"We will, Mom." Nate reassured me. "I know you're attached to Hayley's kids. We wish you could be in Alex's life, too."

That made me a little sad, even though I knew it was true.

Alex finished his bottle and was ready for bed. I gave him a big squeeze and hugged Anna.

"Thank you for dinner. We loved spending time with the three of you." I felt the tears welling up in my eyes. "Take care of this sweet little boy."

Brent hugged her next. "Bye, Anna. Thanks for everything."

Nate drove us back to the hotel. "What time should I pick you up in the morning?"

"Nine o'clock, our rental car should be ready," said Brent. "Then a six-hour drive to Manchester. That is, if we don't get lost."

"You won't, Dad." Nate hugged me and then Brent. "Okay, see you in the morning."

When we got back to our room, Brent turned on the TV, and we got ready for bed.

"Are you sleepy?" Brent looked at me.

"Yes, and no. I had such a good time with Nate and Anna. My eyes are tired, but I have to wind down."

"Me, too. I think I'll watch TV for a little while. If it bothers you, I can turn it off."

"It's fine." I crawled into bed, but I tossed and turned.

I couldn't help but be nervous about tomorrow. It should be a momentous occasion meeting so many Donovans.

I contemplated the days ahead. My prayers were for all my new-found relatives. I prayed I would get along with them, make lasting connections, and relate on some level. After all, they were strangers, and we had no prior relationship.

Amanda had already proved she was accepting. All I could do was pray everyone else would be, too.

I thanked God for taking me on this adventure. For His faithfulness to me in keeping His promises. Trusting Him was something I could do now in any circumstance, even if the outcome took a long time, and I didn't know where it was heading.

Chapter Twenty-Five

The car rental agency was in downtown Altoona, and Nate brought Alex with him to pick us up at nine a.m. We had it prearranged, so all they needed was our signature.

Nate walked around the front of the car when Brent got out. "Thanks for coming out to see us. It's been fun for Alex. I think he got used to you two being here."

Brent stepped toward Nate and gave him a bear hug. "Anna's parents are lucky to see him all the time."

I leaned over and gave Alex a kiss on the forehead. "I love you, little man. We may not see you often, but you're always in my prayers. Be good for Mommy and Daddy."

I climbed out and gave Nate a hug. Tears leaked from the corners of my eyes. "Thank you for taking time off work and spending it with us. This has been a fun trip."

We waved goodbye and went into the rental office and picked up the keys for the car.

Brent put our luggage in the trunk. "Do you have the map?"

I held up the folded paper road map. "Yes. You do know there's a GPS system in the car." I laughed. "Even though we've never been able to figure them out, so I have a map and route planned out."

"I hope we don't get stuck in traffic. It's a workday, so people will be heading home, and we're not familiar with the roads."

The scenery through eastern Pennsylvania was green and lush. Towns dotted the landscape, along with forests.

I looked out the window across the beautiful countryside. "Everything is green here. At home, the bushes are brown this time of year," I said.

"We love the year-round sun in San Diego, but they have all of the rain."

We decided to stop for lunch and found a restaurant off the highway for hamburgers.

"We've been driving for three hours." I showed Brent the map. "We're about halfway there. Here we are and here's our destination."

"We're making good progress," said Brent. "Unfortunately, I don't think we can avoid the traffic. Guess we had better finish eating and get back on the road."

Heading toward Manchester, we crossed over a small portion of New York. As predicted, we encountered a slowdown.

"Now that we're at a crawl, I have a chance to really look around," said Brent. "I like the rural feeling, even here in the city."

I peered around at the scenery, then back down at the map. I didn't want to miss the turnoff.

"Amanda and Peter made reservations for us at the Charles Cheney Inn. It's a bed-and-breakfast. We should probably call them after we get settled. I can hardly sit still." I tapped the map. "We're almost to Manchester."

"It was nice of them to get us a place. I can't wait to meet them."

"Here's the turnoff to town. Now we need to find Hartford Road."

A few minutes later, we found it. "Here's the road to the Inn. Apparently, it has two stone pillars with lights on top. It should be on the right."

"I see them."

The yellow English tudor house was magnificent, the greenery surrounding it beckoned me for morning walks.

Brent parked the car in the front. "Let's go check in, then get our bags."

The front entrance opened to a beautiful entryway.

"Wow, Brent. Look at the beautiful antique furniture, and the wooden floors are gorgeous."

I picked up a pamphlet. "It says here this house was built as a family home in 1864." I looked around. "The current owner has kept the 1800s atmosphere."

A woman stepped out to greet us from the room to our left.

"Hi, I'm Mary. Are you checking in?"

"Yes, we're the Fagianos. Amanda Cleary made our reservation," said Brent.

"Super. Come on in and sign the guest register. Let's see, you'll be staying in the gray room. It's up the stairs, a little to the right. Don't forget to sign up for breakfast."

"Thank you," I said, and we went out to get our luggage.

We headed up the elegant, curving wooden staircase. The spacious gray room had a wrought iron queen bed, red quilt bedspread, and a fireplace with a chair and ottoman.

"This is wonderful," Brent exclaimed. He put his suitcase down and looked out the window. "We can see the koi pond from here."

I set my suitcase on the ottoman and went into the bathroom. "You have to see this. Everything looks original. A little sink, red curtains, a bathtub with a curtain." I laughed. "Here's a small vanity table."

Brent stood at the bathroom door. "Makes you feel as if you're right back in the era it was built. We wouldn't have thought of staying in a place like this. So much better than a hotel."

"I'll call Amanda and let her know we've arrived. Then let's explore."

After my call, we went down to the dining room where there was a long table and chairs.

"Here's where we'll eat breakfast, I think." I picked up a paper menu from the side table along with the signup sheet. "Here are the choices. I'm going for a light breakfast. I don't want my stomach to act up while I'm on vacation. What sounds good to you?"

"Blueberry pancakes, bacon, and juice. Do you want a muffin? They have blueberry."

"Yes, sounds good."

I was fascinated by all the little details of this room. The vases on the mantel above the fireplace, the lace tablecloth. A kitchen was to the left and the parlor to the right.

We wandered through the entryway to the parlor.

"The furniture is so beautiful, and the woodwork is awe-inspiring. There are lots of windows to bring in the sunlight," said Brent. "You can imagine people in their elegant attire back in the day, lounging in this room."

I looked at my watch. "Amanda and Peter will be here any minute. Let's go to the indoor porch area to wait for them."

A few minutes later, they drove up.

I walked right up to Amanda and gave her a hug. "We're so happy to be here. Thank you for arranging this charming place for us to stay." I turned to Peter and hugged him. "It's wonderful to meet you. Being here means so much to me."

Brent shook hands with Peter and enveloped Amanda in a hug.

"Your quick acceptance of Patrish changed her life," Brent told them. "She held on to the hope of finding her biological family, and you provided the entire family tree."

"DNA doesn't lie. It turned out to be a happy surprise for all of us." Amanda beamed.

"I can't believe you answered all my questions in one day. I found Ron, got to meet him, and now I get to meet all of you."

Peter led us to their car. "We're going to Rocco's for dinner. It's one of our favorite places, we hope you like Italian food."

"We love Italian," said Brent.

We drove the short distance to the restaurant. Rocco's had a nice Italian atmosphere, and the food looked delicious. The rich Italian aromas filled our senses.

I studied the menu. "What do you recommend?"

"The lasagna is excellent. There are lots of pizza choices," said Amanda. "I usually get the stuffed shells. Peter likes the little, individual pizzas."

We liked her suggestions, decided to split the lasagna, and everyone placed their orders.

"Patrish," Amanda added, "I'd like to hear more about your visit with Ron."

"It was surreal to me. We had been talking on the phone for eight months, but being there with him made it all come together. We knew the basics about each other. He spoke a lot about his job through the years on ships. I'm glad there weren't any nervous lapses in our conversations."

The waitress placed the lasagna between Brent and me.

"This smells delicious," I said. She gave us an extra plate to divide it.

Amanda moved her napkin, making room for the stuffed shells, and Peter smiled when his pizza arrived.

"Can you tell us a little more about what's going on tomorrow at the reunion? You have a house on the lake, right?"

Amanda put down her fork. "Yes, Amston Lake. It belonged to my parents. You'll get to meet everyone there."

A huge smile covered my face. "I'm excited. It's a good thing you told them about me last year. They've had some time to get used to the idea of another cousin."

Amanda scoffed. "You'll fit right in."

"This lasagna is the perfect blend of sauce and cheese," said Brent. "How's your pizza, Peter?"

He pulled off a slice, and a long string of cheese connected his piece to the others on the tray. "Cheesy and delectable," he said and took a bite.

We all laughed.

It had been a long day for us, and after finishing our meal, we went back to the Inn.

Peter told us they would pick us up at twelve noon.

We walked back to our room. "We'll have time to walk around in the morning."

We climbed the impressive stairway to our room and unpacked our suitcases, placing our things in the dresser drawers. "Today turned out to be a really great day." I picked up my toothbrush and went to the bathroom.

"This is only the beginning. Saturday's reunion will be a big day for you. Time to get a good night's sleep." Brent put his arm around my shoulders.

He got that right, but will I be able to sleep?

CHAPTER TWENTY-SIX

At seven a.m., my eyes snapped open. Reunion day. Brent woke up at the same time.

"Let's get dressed and go down to breakfast. I'm ready for blueberry pancakes."

I nodded. "Sounds good. Let's go for a long walk after we eat."

The dining room table was set for ten guests. Two other couples were eating their breakfast when we arrived. We had just introduced ourselves when Mary came out of the kitchen.

"Good morning, I hope you slept well. Breakfast will be out soon."

"Thank you," we said in unison.

Mary turned and went back into the kitchen.

"Have a great day," a couple of the other guests called to us as they headed toward the front door.

Brent and I waved to them. "We will. You all have a fun day, too," I said.

Our breakfast arrived, and Brent ate his pancakes with gusto. "Oh boy, this is delicious. Look at the size of the blueberries."

I laughed. "They're huge in my muffin, too. Looks like they came from a farmers' market. Can I have a bite of your bacon? I don't want the whole thing. Only a taste."

He slid his plate over to me, and I pulled off a small piece.

Mary came over to the table. "Are you enjoying breakfast?"

"Breakfast was wonderful. I love my blueberry pancakes. This inn makes me feel like we're reliving the 1800s. The history of this house must be fascinating."

"It is. You should look it up online. You'll get an idea of the history behind the Cheney brothers and the silk factory they established. It was a big deal for this area."

"I looked up the basics before we came. I'd love to learn more. We want to go out by the koi pond and wander around the neighborhood. Thank you for breakfast. We'll put our choices for tomorrow's breakfast on the list before we go outside."

Dressed in shorts and tennis shoes, we strolled out the front door and walked around the back of the Inn to the koi pond. I could see the window to our room from where we stood. Beautiful, tall green trees grew outside a six-foot hedge that surrounded the pond, providing plenty of shade.

I turned around to get a three-hundred-and-sixty-degree view of the landscape. "I wonder if it was this pretty way back in the 1800s. I can imagine the family enjoyed this grassy area and the privacy of the hedge."

Brent agreed. "Let's go check out the other side of the inn. I noticed another road, looks like it makes a big circle."

There were a few other houses set back from the road.

"It's so quiet. All I can hear are birds singing. The houses are huge, and the yards all have rolling, green hills with so much land. I wonder how old they are," I said.

"Pretty old, I think. The farther we go on this road, the more traffic I hear. We're not too far from the downtown area, but you'd never know it by looking around."

We had made a big loop all the way around the inn.

"I'm going to change my clothes before Amanda and Peter pick us up. I only get one chance to make a first impression on my new family." I laughed.

"If they're like Amanda, they don't care how you're dressed. She's very accepting of you the way you are. But I get it. I need to change, too. There's plenty of time before they get here."

"That's true. She is wonderful. I'm getting excited and nervous. I don't want to expect too much from them since we are meeting late in life. Everyone's established, and they all have a history together. I'm the interloper."

"Be yourself. Get to know them as best you can in this short time. It's a new experience for you, and an extension to add to the great family you grew up with."

"I kind of wish Ron could be here. But maybe it would be embarrassing for him. I'm the oops."

CHAPTER TWENTY-SEVEN

Peter and Amanda arrived on time. The day turned out to be warm with few clouds in the sky. Dressed in our shorts and short-sleeved shirts, we were all ready for a fun day at the lake.

Amanda turned around from the front seat. "It will take about half an hour to get to the lake house. We'll drive a little slower, so you can take in the scenery."

"Thank you. We loved our walk this morning, seeing all the green, rolling hills. Everything is so beautiful."

"It's amazing how outside of downtown most of the city feels like country living. Peter and I were both raised here. I can't imagine living anywhere else."

"Summertime is beautiful. The snow is, too, but I can't see myself living in a cold climate," I said.

Peter laughed. "San Diego does have perfect weather year-round. I can see why you'd want to stay there."

"I grew up in Chicago. Some winters were rough. It was my job to shovel snow off the driveway. It seemed to be endless," said Brent. "My parents got tired of the cold and moved to Lake Havasu, Arizona. Talk about a weather change. It was blistering hot in the summer. We were fortunate to move from there to San Diego."

"Wow, one extreme to the other. Moderate weather would have been my choice, too," said Amanda.

"I know how lucky I am to have grown up in San Diego. I enjoy traveling to see other climates, but I don't want to move there."

I looked out the window. "The roads and scenery are impressive here. Tree-lined streets, large lots, everything green. It's very different from where we live. I guess we're city slickers."

"The nice thing about Manchester is you can go from rural to city in a short time. Homes have good sized lots," Peter added.

"We're almost there. How do you feel about meeting everyone?" Amanda inquired.

"I've memorized who's who from the family tree you sent me. I can't wait to meet Donna. It will be easier with the kids, husbands, and wives around as a distraction. I won't be the center of attention."

"They'll all love you."

"Here we are," said Peter. "This is our lake house. We love coming out here."

Amanda leaned forward. "Looks like Shauna, Shannon, and family are here. Jennifer has been staying in the house during her visit. She's our cousin Lynn's daughter."

I was nervous, but I nodded my head. "I'm ready. Here we go."

We entered through the front door. I could see the living room on the right, kitchen straight ahead, and a hallway leading to the bedroom.

"FYI, the bathroom is here." Amanda pointed it out. "The party is on the back deck." She led us outside.

Sitting in the shade was a pretty brunette. She stood and Amanda hugged her.

"This is our daughter Shannon. I'm guessing her husband Brad is down by the lake with their boys, Brenden and Oliver. They're seven and three."

Shannon nodded. "Hi, it's nice to meet you. Yes, the kids are fascinated by the water."

We both said hi, and Brent said, "We're happy to be here. This is a beautiful view of the lake."

Another brunette with startling blue eyes hurried up to us.

"This is my daughter, Shauna," said Amanda. "These are two more grandchildren. Ellie is eight and Braxton is three."

"They're mine." Shauna walked up and ruffled her two children's hair.

"Shauna's husband is Mark," said Amanda. She turned to Shauna. "Where is he?"

We all walked to the deck to sit in the shade.

"He'll be here in a little while," said Shauna. She turned to us. "Welcome to the lake house. Most of the family will be here today, so you'll be meeting a lot of people."

Amanda pointed toward the back door. "Here comes Donna with her son, James, and his wife, Amy. Donna's spending July with them here in Manchester. She lives in Florida."

I turned to see Donna walking toward us. She was petite, with white hair and a big smile.

She walked directly up to us. "Where's Patrish? I've been waiting a long time to meet her."

I left the group and met her halfway. "It is such a pleasure to meet you." I turned to Brent. "This is my husband, Brent."

She enveloped me in a big hug.

"I would've known you anywhere," she said to me. "You look like a Donovan."

Unexpected tears welled up. Her eyes, like mine, were the signature family blue.

I belonged.

She turned to Brent and gave him a hug, too.

Brent hugged her back. "Patrish has been looking forward to meeting you, Donna."

We found a chair in the shade for Donna. At ninety-three, she still seemed spry. Everyone else in the family came up to her to say hello. She appeared to be a well-respected member of the family.

Amanda introduced us to James and Amy.

"The long, lost cousin," James teased. "Welcome to the family reunion. I hope it's not too overwhelming."

"I must admit, it's a lot. Did you know we have the same birthday? November 5. You're one year ahead of me."

"Really, that's interesting."

We shook hands with Amy. "It's great you could join us this year. Our barbecues are always fun."

Amanda nudged my arm. "There's my brother, Michael, sitting in the shade with his son, Nick. I'll introduce you."

As we approached, they stood. Michael and Nick were both tall, with brown hair.

"Amanda's told us a lot about you. Welcome," said Michael.

Brent and I smiled at them as we shook hands. I wasn't sure who I should greet with a hug. I let them take the lead.

Amanda looked around. "Two more cousins to meet. Here comes Conner and Lynn."

Conner gave me a big hug. "So, we finally get to meet the big surprise. You fit right in with the Donovans. Blue eyes and everything. I teased Uncle Ron after I found out about you."

Lynn smiled and hugged me. "You'll get used to my brother's sense of humor. He teases everyone."

I laughed. "I see what you mean about blue eyes. I've never seen so many in one place. All the cousins in the Donovan line. It's a strong gene."

"Let's get a picture of us all together. Brent, will you take it?" Amanda handed him her phone.

I handed him my camera. "Please take one with our camera, too."

"You're a good-looking bunch, everyone say cheese."

"Patrish, I know you wanted some time to talk to Donna. Let's pull chairs up by her in the shade," said Amanda.

We put our chairs close to Donna and leaned in closer to her. "I bet you have interesting stories to tell about your brothers and sister growing up."

"Yes, we all got along very well. Amanda's mom, Evelyn, and your dad, Ron, had a special bond. They backed each other up on every story, even if it wasn't the truth. You couldn't put a wedge between them.

"There's an advantage to living in a smaller town. Evelyn and Joseph were high school sweethearts. Same with Amanda and Peter. We stayed here and raised our families. Ron had different ideas. He spent most of his time traveling. After the Navy, his interest in ships remained and became his career."

"He told me a lot about his jobs. All the places he's seen, traveling around the world. He led an interesting life," I said.

"The perpetual bachelor, or so we thought. It took him a while to get married. Even then, he continued to travel. Have you met his sons, Daniel and Blake, yet? I believe Ron missed quite a few of their birthdays and Christmases."

"No, I haven't met them yet. Amanda told me Blake doesn't come to the East coast reunions very often. Ron indicated Daniel has spent this last year traveling. I hope I get to meet them."

I looked around to find Brent. He was sitting with Nick, Michael, and Conner, listening to their conversations. I smiled at him. I didn't want him to feel ignored, but he had a knack for fitting in wherever he went.

Amanda nodded in agreement. "My mom always spoke about how nice it was to have her grandparents living upstairs when she was growing up. She used to go up there as a reprieve when she got disciplined. She loved Thora's Swedish accent. Said she called her lilla du, which means little one."

"Yes, we were close to our grandparents. Grandmother would bake bread every Sunday. The heavenly scent of Braided Cardamom bread floated down the stairs. I'll never forget that wonderful aroma. Her Swedish pancakes were a Saturday morning treat. It's good to keep family close."

Jennifer and James came over to our little group. Jennifer sat next to Donna, and Amanda stood. We saw Amy, Shannon, and Shauna heading into the house.

Brent joined us.

"Looks like we're getting ready to barbecue. I always do the grilling at these events," said Amanda.

"I can be the chef this year. I do it for our parties at home," said Brent.

"We depend on him for it, and he does a good job. It'll give you a chance to visit with everyone." I said, "Of course, he'll need an apron."

"Okay, if you don't mind. Come with me into the kitchen. We'll get you an apron and bring the meat out to put on the grill."

Amanda led him into the house. I took this opportunity to go down by the lake. Mark and Brenden were knee deep in the water, looking at the fish. Peter sat in the shade on a lounge chair.

A gentle breeze blew through the trees. It wasn't too hot if you stayed out of the sun. I took pictures of the back deck and the lake. I climbed up the stairs to the deck and took pictures of different groups of people. My family. It seemed strange; we grew up in different places, went about our lives, never knowing each other.

They didn't know about me, but I had always wondered about my *other* family out there somewhere. Questioning whether I had brothers, sisters, cousins, aunts, uncles. Now I have part of the mystery explained. They were real, and I liked them.

CHAPTER TWENTY-EIGHT

Brent and Amanda came out of the kitchen carrying a tray filled with hamburgers, hot dogs, and chicken. Amanda started the grill, then headed back to the kitchen.

"Shauna, Shannon, and Amy are in the kitchen getting the side dishes ready. Can I put you to work?" she asked me.

"Yes, I'd love to help. Show me what you need done."

The kitchen bustled with activity. My job turned out to be cutting tomatoes for hamburgers. Amanda washed lettuce. Amy worked on the potato salad, while Shannon and Shauna prepared appetizers. Coleslaw, pasta salad, and watermelon were chilling in the refrigerator.

"We have a lot of people to feed. Let's take the appetizers out now. It'll take a while to grill all the meat," said Shannon.

I finished cutting the tomatoes. "I'll take these out and check on Brent."

We set the appetizers on the long table in the shade. It only took an instant for everyone to gather around the plate and claim their favorites. Fresh fruit, cheesy shrimp dip, veggies, crackers, salami, and cheese. Everything looked delicious.

"You have to try Amy's famous shrimp dip, Patrish." Conner filled a cracker and stuffed it into his mouth.

I took his advice and put some of the dip on a cracker. I gave Conner a thumbs up and headed over to Brent at the grill.

"How're you doing? Looks like you're making progress."

"This is a big grill, so it can fit a lot on it, but the chicken will take the longest."

"You must be hot. Do you want something to drink or any appetizers?"

"Thanks, I'll have some lemonade, please."

I found the lemonade and took a glass to Brent.

The enticing smell of grilled food filled the air while everyone devoured the appetizers.

When the burgers and hot dogs were ready, Brent put them on a tray, and I took them inside. They had set up the counter buffet style. All the condiments were out, along with the side dishes.

"Okay, everyone, come and get it," Amanda called out to the back deck.

Plates were loaded with goodies while Brent continued to grill.

I sat next to Conner and Michael. They were discussing motorcycles, and Michael seemed to know about manufacturers and their benefits.

Amanda, Peter, Lynn, and Amy joined us. James took two filled plates over to Donna, handed her one, and sat down next to her. The kids were being chased around the grass by Nick. Getting them to settle down and eat proved to be a challenge.

Amanda stood. "My compliments to the master griller. Thank you, Brent, for taking over for me and doing a fabulous job." She clapped, and all joined in.

Brent raised his spatula and bowed.

Conner laughed. "Without a doubt, Brent can come back next year. The jury's still out on Patrish." Now everyone laughed.

I punched Conner's arm. "Very funny. Brent comes back, I come back. We're a packaged deal."

Conner continued. "We all have stories to tell about Uncle Ron. He taught me to sail on this lake. Did he tell you about all the time he spent traveling?"

"Yes, we got a chance to talk on the phone for about eight months before I saw him in Seattle. He did have quite a few adventures."

The pasta salad tasted delicious. I looked over at Brent with concern. He was missing out on the conversations.

Finally, he could go into the kitchen and load up his plate. He sat down next to me.

"I'm glad you got to meet him. He's a good guy. Always sounds happy to hear from me," said Amanda.

I nodded. "He kept telling me he wanted to come down to San Diego. His health issues prevented it from happening. I decided we needed to go to him. It happened to be my birthday, so I figured it would be a perfect time to go."

Brent took a sip of his lemonade. "He still had more stories to tell Patrish. Her mom was eager to meet him, too, so she went with us. She told him a few stories about Patrish growing up."

"Most of the conversation came from Ron. I think we were all a little nervous, but he had plenty to say." I laughed. "No lulls in the conversation."

Brent and I finished eating, threw our plates away, and meandered down to the lake. There were homes scattered along the water's edge. Directly across the lake were just wild bushes.

I shaded my eyes from the sun. "It would be fun to have a lake house like this. Although in San Diego, a beach house would be more like it."

"It's nice her parents passed the house down to the kids. I'm sorry you never got to meet her mom or dad," said Brent.

"Me, too. Her dad passed away last year. Evelyn died twenty-nine years ago. She was only sixty. Too young."

We trekked back up to the deck. Brent and I helped carry the remaining appetizers back into the kitchen. We wrapped up the leftovers and put them in the refrigerator. Jennifer would have enough food for her entire stay.

Amanda came over to us. "Shannon's invited us to her house. The kids can swim, and we'll have more time to talk. Conner and Jennifer might come over later."

I looked around for Donna. Feeling a little sad, I sighed. "Sounds good. Guess it's time to say goodbye to everyone."

Hugs were given all around. A line formed to say goodbye to Donna. I waited with everyone else.

Donna once again enveloped me in her arms. "This has been a special day for me, Patrish. I know Ron loved finding you. Amanda's kept me in the loop about your talks with him. We're all happy to have you as a part of the family."

"Thank you. This has been wonderful. Meeting all of you, getting pictures, seeing family resemblances."

"We hope to see you again next summer."

"We'd love it, too. You take care." I smiled. "We'll be back."

Shannon and Brad left first. Brent and I got in the car with Peter and Amanda and waved goodbye to everyone.

The road to their house reminded me of a forest. Tall, tree-lined roads, quaint bridges over brooks, and at some points, the trees were so tall they completely masked the sun.

We parked in their driveway and climbed out of the car. "What a big house," I said.

"Wait until you see the backyard. It's perfect for an active family. Let's go through the back gate," said Peter.

The backyard had a huge grassy area and a swimming pool. The veranda covered tables and chairs by the pool, and the upper floor had a deck.

The kids were already in the pool.

I looked over at Shannon. "I love your backyard. It must be pretty in the snow, too."

"Thank you. We like it, and it's such a great place for the kids to play. We also have a boat we can use in the summertime."

Peter's brother, Grady, and his nine-year-old grandson, Keenan, were over, too. Peter and Grady were deep in conversation, and Brenden and Keenan played together in the deep end of the pool, while Oliver stayed in the shallow end. The sounds of the kids' laughter and splashing filled the summer air.

We visited and watched the kids in the pool for about an hour and a half. They decided to get out, dry off, and play wiffle ball. Brent offered to pitch for them. Keenan was at bat, with Brenden in the outfield.

Brent called out, "Okay, Keenan, here it comes. Let's see you blast it."

Smack! The ball went the total length of the backyard, a home run!

"Awesome hit, Keenan. You've really got an eye for the ball and a good bat swing." Brent cheered.

"Way to go, slugger. Sign him up," I yelled.

Brenden batted next. A few strikes and bam, he hit a line drive.

Brent called, "There you go. A hit down the baseline is hard for the infield or outfield to get. You're both good hitters."

Keenan was up again. This one sailed over Brenden's head. Now the boys had our complete attention.

Grady whistled. "That's my boy!"

He turned to me. "He enjoys playing baseball, but soccer is his first love."

"Okay, Brenden. Show us what you can do," said Brent.

Brenden nodded, a look of concentration on his face. Another line drive.

Amanda stood and clapped. "Yahoo, go Brenden!"

Oliver wandered into the infield. Shannon cupped her hands and shouted, "Watch out for the ball, buddy." She turned to me. "I think I'm going to put together a light meal and bring down some drinks."

"We'll help." Amanda gestured to me, and we both followed Shannon inside.

"We'll just do something simple. I have pretzels, crackers, Brie cheese, nuts, and grapes. Mom, the drinks are in the fridge. Help yourself to whatever anyone wants," said Shannon.

I helped warm the Brie and wash the grapes. "Your home is so spacious. I love this big kitchen looking over the backyard. Thank you for having us over."

"You're welcome. It's nice having you here." Shannon handed me a platter for the cheese and crackers.

"It looks like Shauna and family won't make it," said Amanda. "I hoped you'd get a chance to get to know her, too. I guess Conner and Jennifer won't be here, either."

"Patrish, the drinks are in the refrigerator," said Shannon. "Get whatever you and Brent want."

I opened the door and pulled out a Sprite and a root beer.

Amanda got a tray for the food out of the cupboard.

We finished the preparations and took everything back out by the pool.

The air had cooled down, and the sun wasn't as intense. I chose to sit in the warmth and let my skin soak up the vitamin D.

I looked over at Brent. "It looked like you were having fun with the kids. I think they enjoyed it, too."

"It reminded me of the days with Nate and all the practicing we did." He chuckled. "Both boys can really hit. And yes, I had fun, too."

An hour later, Peter asked us if we were ready to go. We said our goodbyes and headed back to the inn.

"We'll pick you up tomorrow at ten for a tour of Manchester. Sleep well." Amanda hugged both of us.

Brent and I climbed the stairs to our room. The inn was very quiet.

"Did you have a good time today, Patrish?"

"Yes, it was wonderful, and I got a chance to talk to most of the family. Sometimes I listened to their conversations without saying a word. It was a comfortable silence." I laughed. "That Conner is a teaser. It's best to be on alert around him."

"I liked them, too. I enjoyed helping with the grilling. No reason Amanda should have to do it and miss out on being with everyone."

"Yes, thank you. You know, it's funny." I flopped down on the bed. "I felt comfortable, but no one asked for my phone number or email address. I doubt I'll be close to anyone besides Amanda and Peter. They're all on the East coast, and our lives are separate. It's okay. I hope we'll be able to come back for another reunion."

"Let's relax tonight, watch a little TV, then call it a night." He sat behind me on the bed and rubbed my back. "You've had quite a day."

I relaxed into the welcome massage.

"Where are we going tomorrow?"

"Amanda said most of the places we'll go will pertain to family, so that will be nice."

"You'll love that. Reaching down deeper into your roots."

I closed my eyes and nodded.

Tomorrow will be an interesting history lesson.

CHAPTER TWENTY-NINE

Sunday morning, we arrived for breakfast at seven a.m. Brent chose French toast, and I had a bowl of fruit. Two other guests were also enjoying their breakfasts.

Mary poured coffee for Brent. "How has your visit been going? You have relatives here in Manchester, right?"

I put my fork down. "Yes, we're having a wonderful time. This morning we're going for another walk, then my cousin is picking us up."

"Did Patrish tell you the story behind our visit here? It's incredible."

"No, do tell." Mary pulled out a chair and sat down.

She listened while I told her about the search for my biological mom, what I uncovered, and how a DNA test led me to find Amanda.

"That sounds like a movie. So many twists, turns, and a great detour. I'm happy for you."

"I've enjoyed finding my birth father's side of the family. I still wish I could connect with someone from my birth mother's family. I have a half sister. Maybe someday it'll happen." I sighed.

Mary expressed encouragement for my quest.

We finished our breakfast and headed out to explore. The sun felt good on my face. We traveled down the driveway we had come in on and turned right this time onto Hartford Road toward the factory.

The rows of red brick buildings had once been the Cheney Silk factory. Amanda had told us how the Cheney's were responsible for a lot of employment in Manchester. This area appeared to be more industrial than the area we saw yesterday.

We made a wide loop, heading back to the inn. We once again waited on the inside porch for Amanda and Peter. After they arrived, I took a picture of them standing in the elegant parlor.

Before going out to the car, Amanda touched my arm. "I have something for you."

She handed me a red box with gold lines around the opening.

Lifting the lid, my hand flew to my mouth, and I gasped. Inside it held a delicate ruby ring. The ruby was oval shaped with a diamond on the top and one on the bottom.

"It belonged to our great-grandmother, Thora. She passed it down to her daughter Alice, who gave it to my mother, Evelyn. I was next in line. I asked Shannon and Shauna if they minded me giving it to you. They both thought it would be special for you to have it."

My vision blurred, tears spilling down my cheeks. I gaped at Amanda, rushing over to throw my arms around her neck.

"I'll treasure this gift forever. Thank you so much for passing this family heirloom on to me. Now I feel even more a part of this family."

We held the hug for a few seconds, savoring our connection. I showed the ring to Brent.

"Try it on," said Brent.

"See, it's a perfect fit. It belongs with you. I'm so glad you like it." Amanda's eyes glistened.

We climbed into the car. Our first stop was the house the Donovan kids had grown up in.

"This is the house where their grandparents lived upstairs. Let's stop, Peter, so Patrish can get out and take a picture."

I snapped the shot. I'd heard great stories about my family living here. Looking around, I wondered in what ways the area had been different back then.

"We'll go to the East cemetery next. My mom, dad, grandparents, and great-grandparents are all buried there."

The cemetery was located in a large, flat area surrounded by homes. Peter guided the car through the winding roads until we found the right spot.

We parked the car, got out, and followed Amanda.

She walked up to a headstone. "These are our great-grandparents, Thora and Alfred."

Both of their names were on the single monument.

I touched her name. "Thank you, Thora, for the beautiful ruby ring passed down through the generations." I could almost hear her say, "You're welcome, lilla du."

Alice and Walter also shared one headstone, as did Evelyn and Joseph. We stood in reverence at their sites.

"This is a pretty cemetery." I shaded my eyes and looked around. "It looks big."

"It is big; fifty-one acres total. The historical society of Manchester has all the facts about how it grew over time. We'll go there tomorrow."

The four of us got back in the car and drove the short distance to Center Memorial Park. We got out and strolled through the park, looking for the Dancing Bear Fountain.

I looked around. "This is a pretty park. Lots of places to walk on windy sidewalks and grassy areas for picnics. Being right in the middle of town, it's perfect on a summer's day."

Peter pointed to a statue. "Here they are."

The Dancing Bears statue stood on top of a five-foot-high fountain that was supported by two concrete circle platforms, each about six inches high. The bronze bears were embracing as if they were dancing.

"Aw, they're cute. Has this fountain been here a long time?" I asked.

"It was given to the park in 1909 by the Cheney family in honor of one of the brothers."

"That's quite a lengthy dance." I laughed.

"Let's go," said Amanda. "There's a special place Peter and I want to take you for lunch. The Shady Glen Restaurant and Ice Cream Parlor. It's a must visit in Manchester, and we need to get there early. It can get crowded at noon."

"They serve hamburgers with fried cheese. You have to try one. They make the best milkshakes around. You'll love it," said Peter.

"Sounds good," Brent and I said in unison.

We pulled into the parking lot of the one-story brick building. The décor inside looked like an old-fashioned ice cream parlor. It had booths and a counter, with stools for seating.

The waitresses wore uniforms from yesteryear, and the waiters wore paper hats.

We found seats and looked over the menus. Brent pointed to a plate at a nearby table.

"I want that." Brent laughed. "I'm going to take Peter's recommendation for the burgers, fries, and chocolate milkshake."

"I knew you'd get the chocolate shake. Will you share your fries with me?"

Brent's eyes narrowed.

"Well, I'm only getting the burger and a soda."

We ordered and got our food in record time. Brent couldn't wait to taste his shake.

I picked at the cheese hanging over the bun of my hamburger and popped it into my mouth.

"Brent, look at this gigantic piece of cheese. It's curling up over the burger."

He took a long sip of his shake. His smile spread from ear to ear.

"My shake is so good. I've never seen fried cheese on a hamburger before."

"This restaurant is well known for it. I'm glad you like your shake, Brent," Amanda said before taking another bite of her burger.

The restaurant began to fill up. Families, couples, singles, everyone in search of a good meal. The atmosphere started getting loud and lively.

"I'm stuffed. Thank you for bringing us here. It's delightful."

"They have the best ice cream here," said Amanda. "Too bad you don't have room for it."

I groaned. "I couldn't eat another bite."

"There are a few more places we want to take you before we go to our house," said Peter.

We drove for a few minutes and stopped in front of a big brick building.

Amanda looked out the window. "This is the site of Nathan Hale Elementary School. Our grandmother, Alice, attended this school the year they had a huge fire. Everyone evacuated, and no one got hurt. It was a wooden structure then, but they rebuilt it, and all the schools after that, with bricks."

"That must have been so scary for the children."

"Yes, my mother passed down stories Alice told her about that day."

We drove to a church with a tall steeple and stopped. The windows contained impressive stained-glass images.

"This is Emanuel Lutheran. Our grandparents attended this church with their children. Swedish immigrants founded it in the 1870s, they enlarged it in 1923."

"Interesting facts. Amanda, you sound like a tour guide." I laughed. "I can tell you were a librarian."

She smiled. "Happy to oblige. Now we'll take you to our home."

We drove down a wide, tree-lined street with large grass front yards and two-story homes. Their home sat on the corner lot.

"It's gorgeous," I said.

The immense house had a detached two-car garage, and lots of grass.

We parked in the driveway and followed them into the house.

We stepped into a beautiful kitchen next to the dining room and into the family room.

Brent looked around. "Impressive on the inside, too, very charming."

Peter opened his hands. "We have plenty of space and can accommodate the grandkids when they want to spend the night."

Amanda looped her arm through mine. "Let's sit in the family room. I have something to give you, Patrish."

"Okay." I shrugged my shoulders and glanced at Brent.

We sat on the couch, and she handed me two DVDs. The label on the outside of one had the title Family Get-togethers 1960-1965. The other one Family 1965-1971.

I gasped. "All the things I missed."

She put a DVD into the player.

When the movie started, Christmas music flowed through the air. Amanda had overlayed the pictures with songs. Although the video contained no voices, their laughter filled my head. In my imagination, I could smell the Christmas tree covered in tinsel. Hear the music, as Amanda's parents danced. The love on the faces of the grandparents smiling down at the young children who danced together pulled me into the celebration.

Amanda identified each family member as they came on the screen. "We had Christmases like this every year. The whole family together."

My eyes were riveted on the video. I let my tears fall, unashamed that my eyes were red, and my face looked blotchy. I'd cried many times over the loss of my biological family. Today, the tears were both happy and sad. The video continued with everyone sitting down to dinner. They said grace before eating.

Amanda handed me some tissues.

"It almost feels like I'm there. I can close my eyes and hear the sizzling potatoes, taste the roast beef, get a whiff of the cinnamon coming out of the kitchen. Christmas music playing in the background. Your mom and dad are a striking couple. Her beautiful blonde hair, his dark hair. Both were very good looking."

"Thank you. They always had fun together. I love seeing them like this."

The video transitioned from opening presents to celebrating Easter. The picture focused on my cousin, Lynn, twirling for the camera in her frilly Easter dress.

I leaned forward, placing my elbows on my knees. "How cute. She's full of energy. It's fun to see the pretty Easter dresses and ties on the men. Special occasions are less formal now."

Amanda pointed to the screen. "Here we are at our summer barbecue. All the adults brought a dish to share. We had a big, grassy area to run around."

Brent laughed. "Look at the closeups of everyone eating corn on the cob. They all have their own, messy styles."

"Unique," I said. "My dad was the funniest corn eater of all time. He'd slap a big slab of butter on the end and gnaw it straight across. Butter dripped down his chin. Brent has seen it. Remembering makes me laugh."

"There's no neat way to do it unless you cut it off the cob and where's the fun in that?" Amanda smacked her lips. "Now we're in November. Look at that turkey."

Amanda's mom took a large, perfectly browned, juicy turkey out of the oven. My mouth watered, imagining the tender meat. Homemade rolls, fluffy mashed potatoes, green beans, and salad were on a buffet table. I could taste it all.

"You ate in style. I love Thanksgiving dinner. It's my favorite meal of the year," I told them.

"Patrish's mom used to make the traditional dinner for us all. When we bought our home, we gave her a break and had everyone come over to our house for dinner. That way, we had all the leftovers." Brent chuckled.

We continued to watch the video. Christmas came around again, then spring. Celebrations of three birthdays came next.

Amanda gestured toward the screen. "Remember, I told you that

Daniel and I have the same birthday? Well, Michael's is one day before ours, so we celebrated them all together."

"I've noticed someone is absent from all these videos. Did Ron miss every celebration?"

"Most of them, but we all loved it when he came home."

"Must have been hard for his wife. Now I see what he told me is true. He was away a lot."

"Peter, will you put in the next DVD?"

"This is Ron's birthday. Now we can see him on the screen."

"I really enjoy seeing how your family interacts. I mean, our family," I said. "I know they're my family, too, but it feels awkward saying it."

Amanda patted me on the arm. "We want you to feel the connection. You can call them your family."

My face turned red, but my smile beamed.

"Now we're getting to everyone as teenagers. I appear in the summer segment," Peter said proudly.

Another Thanksgiving, Christmas, and summer.

"There I am. Oh, to be so young again." He shook his head.

I smiled. "Ah, young love. You two look cute together. You've been a couple for a long time."

"Yes, we have. There's Michael and Sam. They were best friends, as well as cousins. We're all skinny teenagers." Amanda motioned toward the screen.

Brent said, "It's nice to have the memories recorded. My sister, Jackie, converted our films to DVDs, too. I love seeing our family get-togethers. People who are no longer here."

He turned to me. "Patrish, your mom has a lot of films to convert. All your childhood memories are on slides or eight-millimeter movie film. I've seen a few of them."

The DVD came to an end. "These are for you. Like I said, we want you to feel the connection." Amanda handed me the two DVDs.

"We've enjoyed seeing how you celebrated through the years. Patrish will want to watch it over and over," said Brent.

I twisted Thora's ring on my finger. "Thank you. This is the second great gift you've given me today."

Peter clapped his hands together. "Okay, how about ordering pizza for dinner? We have a place we love to order from, and we'll have it delivered."

Brent and I looked at each other and nodded.

"We'll eat on the back covered patio. Do either of you want a beer?" Amanda asked, heading into the kitchen.

Peter phoned in the order. We got four beers out of the refrigerator, picked up plates and napkins, and headed to the back patio.

"We've had a busy day today," said Brent.

I stretched my arms over my head. "Busy, but relaxing. I can't believe we fly home tomorrow."

"We still have more of Manchester to show you. Oh, Peter, there's the doorbell. Pizza is here."

Peter brought the box out to the patio, and we each took a slice.

"Yum, pepperoni. This is very cheesy," I said, pulling my piece out of the box, as a long string of cheese oozed off the edge.

"It's quiet and peaceful here," Brent commented between bites of pizza.

"Yes, it's special on summer evenings. Warm breezes, watching the sunset," said Amanda.

We ate in contented silence. You could hear the muffled sound of families going down the street. Kids playing, and parents calling kids in for dinner.

We watched the sunset over the hills, then took our plates and the leftover pizza into the kitchen.

"We'll take you back to the inn now. Rest up, tomorrow's another big day."

Amanda put the pizza in the refrigerator.

"More Manchester history," said Peter. "You'll be experts on the subject."

They dropped us off outside the inn, with the promise to pick us up at nine a.m.

Climbing the stairway to our room, Brent commented, "Have you noticed we don't run into any of the other guests? We're gone all day, but where do they go at night?"

"It does seem strange. We only see them at breakfast. They must be as busy as we are."

Lying in bed, I soaked up every memory of the last two days. I never wanted to forget the sights and sounds of this journey. The faces of this family I never knew.

CHAPTER THIRTY

I woke up early. Our last day in Manchester would be busy. I got out of bed and took a shower in the old-fashioned shower tub. The thin pipes for the shower ran up the side of the wall in keeping with the original Victorian design. There were a few modern updates, but I liked pretending to be showering in 1880.

Brent had already started packing his bag.

After I dried my hair, we went down to breakfast. Brent munched on his French toast, and I popped pieces of cranberry muffin into my mouth. We were alone at the table.

Mary served us coffee and asked, "Have you enjoyed your stay in Manchester?"

"It's been great. Patrish's family welcomed us with open arms. We'll finish seeing the sights today."

"I love this inn." I set my water glass on the table. "You've done a great job here. I'm glad they made it a designated National Historic Landmark."

"I'm glad you like it. What time will you be leaving today?"

"We'll be out by two p.m. Our plane leaves at four. This morning, we're going for our last walk around this area," said Brent.

We thanked Mary for breakfast and headed left on Hartford Road toward Main Street. Turning on Main Street, a large, brick building, the Bennett Academy appeared on the right. Up and down Main Street were small shops. We passed a Historic Downtown Manchester sign.

I looked around. "This is quaint. I like the small-town feel of this street. Two lanes each way, traffic lights, but not too congested."

"There's something wonderful about small towns. Your family must love it, too. They settled here and never left."

We wandered a few blocks, then turned around. We didn't want to be late for our last big tour day.

Half an hour later, we were on our way to Cheney Hall. The elegant building was a brick Victorian structure with three arches at the entrance, and well-manicured lawns surrounding it.

Amanda led us in. "I'll give you a brief history of this place. It was built as a theater and cultural community facility for Manchester in 1867. Back then, they had productions, musicals, parties, and balls. It's still used for local live shows."

We stepped into a large room. Shiny wooden floors, a high ceiling, and red drapes wrapped around the stage. The room had a rich history.

A gentleman approached us. "I can take you on a tour, if you'd like."

"Yes, we'd love that," I answered.

He smiled. "My name is John."

Peter and Amanda sauntered behind us as we followed John. He took us backstage where the actors got ready for their roles. We saw posters from past performances and props. They had performed some of my favorite musicals on this stage. *Carousel, Fiddler on the Roof, Guys and Dolls.*

John continued. "The hall has a long history here in Manchester. It was designated a National Historic Landmark Building in 1978. A few years later, it was given to the town of Manchester and became known as The Little Theater of Manchester. We still put on performances."

"My dad had been involved in theater. He loved to perform," said Amanda.

"I remember you telling me about it. I was in a few productions in high school. Chorus only, nothing major, but I loved it. I must get my love of being a ham from your side." I laughed.

The tour ended, and we thanked John. Our next stop would be the Manchester Historical Center. We drove up and stopped at another large, brick building.

"The center came about to preserve and educate everyone about the rich history here in Manchester," Amanda explained as we walked through the front door.

A man came around the counter and approached us.

"Hi, I'm Brad, one of the docents here at the Historical Center. Would you like a tour?"

"Yes, please. This is our first time in Manchester," I said.

He showed us some of the silk machines used at the factory and an area where anyone could come to look up old directories, high school yearbooks, and old booklets.

"This is fascinating. It's nice they decided to preserve the history of this area," said Brent.

"The Cheney Silk factories were responsible for a large number of employees here in Manchester. Some of our relatives worked there, too, Patrish," Amanda added.

"I'm intrigued that our family grew up here, Amanda. This helps us get a feel for how it was back in our grandparents' day."

The tour ended in the bookstore. We thanked Brad and browsed for a little while. There were displays of old photographs, books on local history, maps, T-shirts, cookbooks, and mugs, all displaying Manchester's proud history.

"This has been fun. I learned a lot about this little community. It helps me feel more connected to all of you. Thank you, Peter, for chauffeuring us around. We've been able to see quite a bit."

"I'm glad you enjoyed it. Our last stop will be Filomena's for lunch. It's back on Main Street. They have every kind of pizza you can think of, salads, burgers, a wide variety of cuisine," said Peter.

"Here we are, back on Main Street," I said. "We came down this street for a little bit this morning, but we didn't come this far."

We found a place to park and entered a green building with a green and white awning.

Once seated, we received our menus. "I've eaten too much already on this trip. I don't want to sit on the plane with a big lump in my stomach. I'm going to go with tortellini soup."

"I agree. The gorgonzola chicken salad sounds good to me. We still have a long trip ahead of us," said Brent.

Peter and Amanda also ordered salads. After we ate, the four of us made our last trip back to the inn.

Parking in the driveway, Amanda got out and opened the trunk. "I have something for you, Patrish. Some souvenirs from your stay here."

She handed me a bag. "You've given me a lot already. An heirloom, precious memories on DVDs, and a whole family."

I opened the bag.

"A Dancing Bear T-shirt! This is great." I pulled out the first book.

"The books are about history. The *Manchester Remembers* book is a memorial book honoring the residents who served in World War II. Look at pages twelve and ninety-one. Our grandfather, Walter, is mentioned and my dad's brother, too."

The next book, *The Miracle Workers'* was all about the silk factory. "Look at the pictures on the note cards, Brent. All the styles they had back then. What a kick!"

Brent laughed and said to Amanda and Peter, "You've been great hosts. Patrish will never forget this trip. Meeting all her family, seeing the town where everyone grew up. We really appreciate all you've done for us."

I hugged Amanda, and we rocked back and forth. "Thank you so much. I hope we'll make it out here again for another reunion. You're always welcome to come visit us in San Diego."

Brent and Peter hugged, then we switched hugging partners. My smile mixed with tears. It was time to load up our car, drop it off at the airport, and catch our plane home.

I waved goodbye, and I stood a little taller. The broken pieces of my circle were closing one by one.

Chapter Thirty-One

On Mother's Day 2018, I had many things to be grateful for. I love the closeness Mom and I share. Hayley had become a wonderful mom. We laughed at how God never gives you more than you can handle. She kept wondering why He thought she could handle triplets. Especially, when all three were crying at once. Nevertheless, I adore her children.

Little Alex continued to grow fast. Nate and Anna had busy lives in Pennsylvania. If only they lived closer. It would have been fun to have all four grandkids in San Diego. Being a grandmother proved to be the best role possible.

At church that Sunday, our pastor's wife, Valerie, and daughter Ann Marie led the service. We were reminded of our special roles in God's plan and how by blessing others, we become blessed. Ann Marie spoke about the resources our church offers for moms, including Tuesday Bible study and opportunities to volunteer. She also mentioned the importance of a praying mom and to never underestimate the power of prayer in our children's lives, no matter their age.

We were reminded that our mothers are human, capable of flaws and mistakes. Today was a day for forgiveness. Ann Marie asked us to close our eyes, think of any broken parts in our relationship with our moms, any old wounds, and pray to forgive them.

Nora popped into my mind. I'd never be able to have a conversation with her or heal past hurts. But I could forgive her. I thought I had moved past all the devastation, yet I still cried watching TV shows depicting happy adoption reunions.

As I sat there, I prayed and forgave her, releasing all the bad feelings I'd kept inside. It was time to set myself free.

I opened my eyes at the end of prayer time and wiped the tears off my cheeks. My lips quivered and broke out into a broad smile. I let out a long sigh.

"You look peaceful," Brent said on the ride home.

"I am. I forgave Nora. I hadn't realized how much it held me down."

For the next two weeks, my steps were lighter, my smile broader. I loved going to Ancestry and visiting Amanda's family tree. She added mine and Brent's names, and Nate and Hayley, along with their kids.

On June 1, I received an email from her.

> I got a message from someone on Ancestry and wanted to contact you right away. Here's the message:
>
> *I'm working on my family tree, and I have been notified Nora Long is also on your family tree. Why is she there?*
>
> I responded with caution and asked if she was a relative of Nora's. She answered yes, so I told her Nora isn't related to me, but a relative of someone I know. I wanted to let you know, Patrish, she's asking about it. Her message board says her name on Ancestry is KC. How do you want me to respond to her?

My breath caught in my throat. KC? Did I dare to hope or would I get a door slammed in my face?

> Those are Katie's initials, Nora's daughter. Sounds like you both were being cautious. You can pass on any

information you want about me. I don't know how she'll respond. Back in 2005, the family didn't want anything to do with me. Don't be surprised if this doesn't go anywhere.

"Okay, I'll see how it goes."

A few minutes later, Amanda responded that Katie had sent her this message:

I think I know who this person might be. I've wanted to get in touch with her for a long time. Can you connect us?

Amanda answered,

We did it. She wants your email address. I'm happy for you. This is fantastic news.

She sent me Katie's email address. I jumped in the air and shouted, "Yes!" which brought Brent running into the room.

"All this dancing and shouting must mean something good happened. What's going on?"

I waved my hands in the air, laughing and spinning around in circles. "Katie found Amanda on Ancestry." I read Brent both Katie and Amanda's conversation.

"Now I have her email. After thirteen years, we've found each other. She wants to connect. Two weeks after I forgave Nora, God delivered Katie."

Happy tears flowed down my cheeks, and Brent wiped them away. "This is a wonderful gift."

"Where do I start? What should I say? I don't want to make her feel bad. The way everything happened in 2005 left me speechless. I've got to get right on this."

I gave Brent a big bear hug and sat down at the computer to compose my email.

Hi Katie. I don't even know where to begin. Thank you for sending your email to Amanda, so I can contact you. As you may guess, I have a lot of questions to ask you. I hope you're okay with giving out information about your family. Email me back and let me know how you feel about all this. Can't wait to hear from you. Patrish

The response came quick.

Hi Patrish. I'm sorry I couldn't contact you when I found out about you in 2005. I have no problem telling you about my family. I've been thinking about how to contact you ever since Mom passed away in March 2007. You can ask me anything. I pray you have a loving family. Katie

"Brent, she's willing to tell me about Nora and herself," I called out to him. "I'm going to ask her for the one thing I've been longing for the most. A picture of Nora."

Katie—I'm glad you're willing to share with me. I'd like a picture of your mom. I've always wondered what she looked like. I had a wonderful upbringing.

I went on to describe the family I grew up with and Brent, Hayley, and Nate.

She emailed me a picture of Nora and Ross. I printed it, and I took it to Brent in the living room.

"I'm not sure I see any resemblance. Do you?"

"Maybe a little," he responded, holding the picture.

More emails from Katie.

They took the picture right after they were married. Sometime between when you and I were born. I look like my dad. Do you look like Mom? I hope this helps you feel a little closer to her. Please send me a picture of you. Oh, and here's my phone number and address. Send me yours, too.

I couldn't stop staring at the picture. Sixty-two years and here she is. She looked happy and nice. Tears filled my eyes. Our relationship wasn't meant to be. I knew I had the next best thing with Katie. I couldn't wait to hear her stories.

This is beyond amazing. Thank you for the picture. Now send me one of you, too. It's hard to tell if I look like her. Maybe a little. Here's my picture. What do you think? Here's my address and phone number. – Patrish

This is eerie. You look exactly like Mom. I'm going to call Janine right now, and we're going to come out and see you. This is too incredible to share over emails. I'll let you know what we decide. Are there any days that are not good for you? Love, Katie

Katie, fantastic! I'm so excited. No conflicts coming up this summer. You and Janine can stay here. We have a second bedroom. We can stay up late and talk. We have a lot to learn about each other. Can't wait to hear back from you. – Patrish

I ran into the living room. "They're coming here. She can't wait any longer, either. She's checking with Janine, then we can find a date that works for everyone."

I put my hand over my racing heart. I jumped when the phone rang. It was Katie, and she and Janine were excited to come. We made plans for them to arrive on August 8.

This was going to be the best summer ever.

CHAPTER THIRTY-TWO

"What time do we have to leave for the airport?" asked Brent. "Their flight gets in at 5:30 this evening. We'll be fighting traffic both ways. They're bringing carry-on luggage. I told them we would meet them outside baggage claim. I'll check to see if their flight is on time before we leave."

"It takes half an hour. We should add fifteen to twenty minutes more for traffic."

I paced around the house, glancing at the clock every five minutes. Brent watched me with an amused smile. I shook my hands out and took deep breaths.

"Okay, it's 4:45. The flight is arriving on time. Let's roll."

Fifteen minutes later, we crawled along with the freeway traffic.

"Don't worry, if we're late, you can call them and let them know," said Brent. "They can wait out front for us."

I crossed and uncrossed my arms. "Yeah, I sure hope we all get along."

"It's strange to think you've never seen them before and have to get their pictures for recognition."

"I know. I could've walked right past them without a clue. I have their faces memorized now."

"Okay, terminal one. I'll have to get over two lanes for baggage claim. We made it here in an hour."

My heart was pounding. "I hope we don't have to circle around and around. It's a hassle when there's no place to stop by the curb."

Brent found a spot and pulled right up to the curb. He didn't say anything, he just smiled.

I jumped out and searched the crowd of arriving travelers.

I gasped. "There they are!"

I caught their attention and ran up to them.

Katie and Janine, here in San Diego.

Katie and I embraced.

"Are you real?" I asked her through tears.

"Yes." She hugged me tight.

I turned to Janine. "I'm happy you came, too." I hugged her, and then we had a group, hold on for your life, hug. Tears streamed down our faces.

"C'mon, the car is over here."

Brent opened the back of the car, then he hugged each of them and took Katie's bag. "This has been a long time coming. Your being here means everything to Patrish."

Janine handed her bag to Brent. "We're happy to be here. As soon as we found you, Mom decided we had to come visit. This is important to us, too."

They climbed into the back seat, and we headed home.

I turned around to look at them and asked, "Your husbands were okay with you coming out here? Janine, I know you have four kids."

"Yes, my husband handles most of the kids' activities, anyway. I travel for work. My leaving doesn't change the schedule."

"Katie, Philippe didn't mind?" I asked.

"No, he knew the importance for all of us. He wants to meet you all, too."

"Do you have any tourist-type things you want to do while you're here? San Diego has a lot of great places to see," said Brent.

"We want to meet your mom, Patrish, and walk on the beach. Whatever you want to do, we're right there with you," said Katie.

"Mom invited us over for lunch on Friday. She wanted to give us some time to get to know each other and bond. You'll love her. She's kind, funny, and supportive through every aspect of my search. She told me she would help in any way she could."

Katie leaned forward in her seat. "I'm looking forward to it. Anyone who adopts four kids, loves them unconditionally, and chooses you is wonderful to me."

Janine smiled. "I agree."

The ride home went by fast. We were all curious about each other's lives. Brent pulled into our condo parking lot, and we climbed out. He opened the liftgate in the back of the car. We got their bags out and headed toward our unit. Brent parked the car in the garage.

"This is a nice complex," Katie commented, catching her breath as we climbed the stairs to our unit. "You get your exercise going up and down these stairs every day."

"Yes, we like the upper units better. They have vaulted ceilings. We don't mind the stairs. They keep us in shape. I only have trouble when my hands are full of heavy grocery bags."

I unlocked the door and let them in. "Your room is here to the left, go ahead and put your bags down. Here's the bathroom. I'll give you the two-cent tour. It's not big, but perfect for us."

I gave them the grand tour, and we settled on the couches in the living room. Brent came in and sat down with us.

"I like this unit," Katie said, looking around. "It feels comfortable and has big windows."

"We can eat out on the patio tomorrow. We don't have a spectacular view, but there's a big grassy area in the back we like to call our backyard. Across the street is the community center. It has several swimming pools, a weight room, and a spa. Brent and I will take you to see it tomorrow."

"Sitting here in the light, I have to tell you, Patrish, you look exactly like Gram." Janine looked wide eyed. "I'm sort of freaking out. You move like her, have the same expressions. Mom and I don't look like her at all. I always wanted to have similarities to her. Looks like you got all her genes."

"I was thinking the same thing," said Katie. "It's uncanny. You weren't around her to pick up any of the gestures, but there they are. You have her build, her eyes, but most of all, her smile."

I raised my eyebrows. "Seems strange to me. I never looked like anyone growing up. Of course, I don't look like my adopted family. I never even saw any strangers who looked like me. Now I know where I got my features."

Janine leaned back on the couch. "She and I were close. I loved spending time with her. She had class and taught me a lot about life."

I looked over at Katie. "I have to tell you. You have the most beautiful green eyes I have ever seen. Who else in your family had green eyes?"

"Grandma, Mom's mom had the same shade of green," she replied. "I didn't get Mom's height. I'm only 5'2" tall. Janine's closer to her in height. I have all my dad's features. I think you and I have the same nose, Patrish."

"I think we do, too. Janine got the gene for blue eyes. Everyone I met on my birth father's side had blue eyes. It must be a strong gene since both of my parents had them."

Brent stood. "Let's get a picture of the three of you marking this special occasion."

All three of us handed Brent our phones. We lined up with Katie on my left and Janine on my right.

"Say sisters," Brent said with a big smile. He took a picture with each of our phones, then handed them back to us. "Okay, check them to see if they turned out."

Katie looked at her camera. "These are great, Brent, thanks."

We returned to our spots on the couch.

I turned to Katie. "Think about all the ways our lives would have been different if we'd grown up together. Two girls, close in age. I bet we would've caused trouble."

"I don't know. I wasn't a troublemaker." Katie frowned. "Were you?"

"No. But our families had different dynamics. You were an only child. I had two brothers and a sister. Maybe one of us would've talked the other into mischief."

"Could be. Poor Mom. She may very well have had her hands full."

"Double trouble." I laughed.

"None of us would be where we are today," said Janine. "I might not even be here. Aunt Patrish's kids either. Or Uncle Brent. We'd be off on another timeline."

"Endless possibilities." I sighed. "I do think about what it could have been like to meet Nora, of course, but your grandparents, too. I don't know what to call them. They're our grandparents, technically. I feel awkward calling them mine."

Katie said, "I called my grandpa Tutu. It's Hawaiian for grandparent. My grandmother I called Grandma. I grew up in Texas but spent my summers with them. They lived by the beach. Tutu taught me how to play golf, and Grandma loved to shop."

"I'm glad you were close to them," I said. "Grandparents can be an important influence on kids."

"They were the best. I still miss them."

"I can't believe Tutu and I shared the same birthday. I bet he didn't consider me a happy birthday present." I laughed.

Katie said, "It wasn't your fault."

"No, but I imagine they hoped my arrival would come on another day."

"Mom became close to her grandparents, and I stayed close to mine," Janine said. "I loved Gram and Grandpa. She taught me about being a lady. She loved wearing pearls and cardigans. To me, she appeared both elegant and fun."

I put my hands over my mouth. "Guess what? I think every sweater in my closet is a cardigan. It's heartwarming to hear all the stories. It makes her real to me. Not a character I made up in my head. Although, I did do a bit of fantasizing about her in my time."

I could tell by their yawns the time difference was catching up to them. We fixed their bed in the guest room, hugged, and said goodnight.

We had two more full days together.

CHAPTER THIRTY-THREE

Katie and Janine were still on East coast time, and I heard them talking at six a.m. I couldn't wait for the day's activities.

I knocked on their door and bounced in with a cheery, "Good morning, girls. I hope you slept okay. Couch beds aren't the most comfortable."

Janine giggled. "We were wound up last night. It took a little while to fall asleep."

"Exhausted and excited," Katie agreed.

"Let's get dressed, have breakfast, and plan our day," I said.

I tiptoed around our bedroom, trying not to wake Brent. We all met in the kitchen where I started coffee for them.

"You don't drink coffee?" Katie asked, her mouth dropping open. "How do you wake up in the morning?"

"I never liked the taste. It smells good, though. Do you want cereal, toast, toaster waffles, or something else?"

Katie looked at Janine. "Only toast for us, thanks," and Janine nodded.

I popped two pieces of bread in the toaster oven. "Next question. Raspberry jam, strawberry jam, peanut butter, or avocado?"

"Avocado," they voiced in unison.

"What are you going to eat?" Janine asked.

"This is too early to be hungry. I'm not much of a breakfast eater."

Toast and coffee in hand, we sat at our round dining room table.

"Let's talk about what we should do today. I was thinking we could go down to the boardwalk in South Mission Beach. It's a long stretch of sidewalk along the ocean. We'll need to go early. Parking is always an issue."

Katie smiled. "We're ready to go anytime."

"Later, Brent and I can show you the community center."

We made small talk while they finished their breakfast. I had one big question I wanted to ask Katie.

"Katie, I need to ask you how it went when you got the letter from Fact Finders about me. I couldn't help being concerned about your reaction."

She put down her coffee cup. "It shocked me. The letter described my family perfectly, including the business my grandparents owned. I called Mom and blurted out, 'Is it true?' She didn't want to admit it."

"The proof turned out to be undeniable," Janine added. "Neither one of us could believe it."

"Finally, Mom admitted it. I asked her if Dad knew. She answered yes, she told him before they were married. She said she didn't know if you were a boy or girl, and the adoption had been arranged for you to go to your new home right after your birth."

I swallowed hard. "I need to let you know. That's not how it happened. She gave me the name Diana Donovan. I was placed in foster care until my adoption. It must have been hard for her to tell you about her circumstances."

"She had a best friend named Diana. I wonder if she named you after her. She felt pressured to tell us about it after the letter. That must be why she made up that part of the story."

"It's a big secret to carry around for all those years. I worried about how it would affect all of you. And who in the world is Jay Hughes? Did she hire a lawyer?"

Katie and Janine looked at each other and started laughing.

"What's so funny?" I asked, wide eyed.

Katie covered her mouth, trying to regain her composure.

"You'll never believe this," she declared, still laughing. "He's Janine's husband. I can tell by the look on your face you didn't see that coming."

Janine cleared her throat. "Gram asked him to call the company. She wanted a name unrelated to the Bower name. Someone sounding official."

"We're sorry she reacted in such a negative way." Katie patted my shoulder. "I would've called you right away. I guess she couldn't deal with it."

"I hope you don't hate us for what happened," Janine muttered in a small voice, her smile turning into a frown. "We were respecting Gram's wishes."

"I can't believe it." I shook my head. "To be honest, for years his name struck terror in my heart. Not knowing his relationship to the family, the gruffness of his request. 'No contact, by phone or writing. They want nothing to do with this person who instigated the search.' Since I know it's your husband, Janine, it is kind of humorous."

"At first, I wondered if maybe you needed medical attention or info," Katie stated. "I became concerned when she handed it over to Jay. Like Janine said, we honored Mom's decision."

"It makes sense. I'm glad to finally know the details. It drove me crazy for years. I didn't want to think bad thoughts about all of you. Everything came to a sudden halt. I worried about your opinion of me. Appearing out of nowhere, upsetting your mom. I hope I didn't put a strain on your relationship with her."

"No, we knew she had always been a private person. We decided not to bring it up again. We have Ancestry to thank for it all coming out. Mom never imagined we would ever connect." Katie laughed.

I shrugged. "God had a plan. He brought us together at the exact right time. Things happen for a reason. It turned out to be a long wait for me, but worth it."

"I know His hand held us through it," Katie replied, taking a sip of coffee. "I recently renewed with Ancestry and began working on the family tree. Putting Mom's name on it and seeing Amanda had added it to her tree brought us all together."

"It answered my prayers. After your mom said no contact, I kept thinking how great it would be to have you. Hear stories, see pictures. Now I have the works."

"A winning situation all the way around," said Janine.

I could hear Brent moving around the bedroom. We decided the time had come to get ready for the beach. I gave them sunscreen and floppy hats. When Brent came out, we told him of the plans for the day.

"Sounds perfect. I'll eat a quick breakfast, then get ready. What time do you want to leave?"

"Nine o'clock. We'll get to the parking lot at Mission Beach at nine thirty. There should be plenty of spaces available then. It's going to be another beautiful, amazing day in San Diego."

CHAPTER THIRTY-FOUR

W̲e found a parking place by Belmont Park. We left our beach chairs in the car, deciding to walk along the boardwalk.

"There's something special about the smell of the ocean. Don't you love the beach?" Katie asked, taking a deep breath. "Mom loved the beach, which is one reason she loved Hawaii so much."

"The smell, the sights, the sounds, seagulls circling. Yep, I love it, too." I lifted my face to the sun. "Growing up, we came here to South Mission a few summers and spent a week here. What a treat for us. Riding our bikes up and down the boardwalk, spending all day on the beach, playing in the waves. My mom had a hard time keeping track of the four of us. There were a lot of scruffy characters hanging out here, too."

"You know, I recognize this place," Katie said, looking around at the homes along the boardwalk. "I remember coming down here with my parents. San Diego was a fun place to visit."

Janine stared out at the waves. "We don't get to the beach often living in Georgia. It's invigorating down here."

"We live close and don't get here often enough," said Brent.

We strolled for a while and decided to sit on the wall and watch the people go by. Some were setting up their umbrellas on the beach.

Others were riding their beach cruisers on the boardwalk, forcing the foot traffic to jump out of their way.

I scooted back on the wall and let my feet dangle over the edge. "I remember being fascinated by all the people. We had to dodge roller skaters and bikes. We tried walking on the wall but couldn't keep our balance. One time, when I was about ten, my brother Blake hopped up on the wall. At seven, he wanted independence and didn't want anyone to help him balance. Suddenly, he lost his footing and fell off the wall, landing on his back. Fortunately, he landed on the sand. I had been a few steps behind him. My mom didn't see him fall because she was ahead of us. A lady ran up to us after seeing him fall. She got down on her knees to make sure he wasn't hurt. I came running up to find him lying in the sand. She asked if he was my brother, and I told her yes and yelled for Mom. I'm glad he didn't land on the sidewalk. Turns out he didn't get hurt."

Katie's smile froze. "Wait a minute? You were ten. You're talking about the summer of 1966? We were down here that summer for a few days. I would've been nine. I remember Mom helping a kid who fell off the wall. Dad and I were on the beach a few feet away. Your brother's the one who fell in the sand?"

My legs stopped swinging. "You mean Nora's the one who stopped?" I asked in disbelief. "I saw her, talked to her? We were face-to-face. I remember her pointing out her husband and daughter on the beach. After we checked on Blake, we left, saying how nice she'd been. I don't believe this."

"Here you are, almost in the same spot," said Brent. "Funny how things work out."

"How incredible." Janine shook her head.

I jumped off the wall, throwing my hands in the air.

"I wish her face had stayed embedded in my memory. I don't recall anything specific. I only felt concern for Blake. A monumental moment unrealized. I'd love to go back there and soak it in. Who could have guessed we'd ever run into each other...?"

"I don't remember any specific details either. I saw your family and looked right at you. You'd think our skin would have tingled or something," Katie said, rubbing her chin.

We continued our walk to the end of South Mission, turning around to head back on the sand. We removed our shoes, swinging them in our hands with each step. The sand felt cool down by the water, squishing between our toes.

"Did you ever go to Belmont Park when you came down here?" I asked Katie, as we once again approached the park.

"No, it wasn't in good shape back in the sixties. The roller coaster loomed high above everything else, but Mom didn't like the looks of the people hanging around."

"We weren't allowed in there, either. The ocean and playing on the beach were always the big draw for us," I told her.

"Does anyone want to go on the roller coaster now?" asked Brent.

I shook my head. "That rickety old thing gives me a headache."

"No, I don't want to, either," said Janine.

"The beach is getting crowded. Should we head out, take a drive down Mission Boulevard?" asked Brent.

I looked over at him. "Okay. Mission Beach is a typical beach town. Lots of fun shops. It's too early for lunch. Let's cruise Mission Boulevard and head back to our place."

"It's crowded today," Brent noted. "Summertime gets crazy down here. We get overrun by Zonies and tourists from all over."

Janine gave him a puzzled look. I laughed.

"Zonies are tourists from Arizona. It's too hot there, so they come here for the summer. If you look around, you'll see lots of Arizona license plates."

When we got home, we walked across the street to the community center. They were impressed by the variety of activities members could participate in.

Back at the condo, we relaxed, and Janine told us fun stories about her younger days, with Katie adding her take on things. We laughed and smiled as if we had always been together. At noon, Brent took our sandwich orders and went to pick up lunch.

"Do you have a baby book or any pictures of when you were growing up?" asked Janine.

"Yes," I answered, "right here in this hall closet." Dragging out my boxes of photo albums, I found the ones from when I was little. "Here's my baby book. Look at those rolls of baby fat. I look bald here. As a towhead, I had fine, blonde hair."

"Neither Janine nor I looked like you as babies. Your mom is beautiful. She looks like a movie star."

"Brent and I think so, too. In this other album, I have pictures of all our Christmas cards. We took family photos every year."

"It's fun to look back. I don't have this many pictures from growing up. I sent you some of them, right?" Katie asked.

"Yes. I love to see your, well, our whole family. Even the grandparents."

We were looking through our wedding album when Brent returned with lunch. He distributed the sandwiches and drinks. We cleaned off the patio table and sat outside on the balcony. Brent and I talked about our wedding. Janine and Katie told us about theirs.

Katie took a sip of her drink. "I don't have any pictures of Mom and Dad's wedding I could show you."

"No problem. I love all the pictures you sent." I pulled out my phone and scrolled through my pictures. "Here's one where she looks exactly like me. I make that same face. A kind of irritated, get this over with look. I freaked out when I saw it. Could've been me."

"I can't even tell you all the ways you look like her," said Janine. "It's like having her back again." She took a bite of her sandwich.

"Speaking of that, I hope you don't mind sharing with me how she died. I went into shock when I saw she died in 2007. Last thing I ever expected to see. We even got a copy of the death certificate, but it was hard to decipher."

Katie put down her sandwich. "We were all shocked, too. She had always been healthy, walked every day. One day, she went out on her walk, stepped off the curb, and had to jump backward as a car approached. The heel of her foot caught on the curb, and she fell on her back, hitting her head on the concrete sidewalk. She had a hematoma, and they operated on her the same day. It took away all her mobility, speech, and cognitive thoughts. My dad had to take care of her until we put her in a nursing facility. She had a long fight but succumbed to her injuries."

I looked down at my hands. "That is so sad. I didn't figure it out from reading the death certificate. I'm sorry it happened to her. Being healthy one day and disabled the next. How awful for all of you."

"Yeah, we had a hard time. We were far away, and I couldn't help my dad. Putting her in the facility seemed the only thing he could do. We had her cremated and scattered her ashes at sea ourselves."

"When did your dad die?"

"In 2015. His death turned out to be hard for different reasons. Not having your parents alive is strange. You still want to talk to them about things going on in your life. I'm glad your mom is still alive. And you have your birth father, too."

"We'll go see Mom tomorrow. Did I tell you about meeting my birth father, Ron? We made the trip up to Seattle because traveling is hard for him. I loved getting to see him face-to-face. We had a lot of long telephone conversations, but in person is better."

"I'm glad you were able to meet him. What did you think, Brent? Does she resemble him, too?"

Brent laughed. "There is some resemblance. The shape of their faces and the dark blue eyes."

"My mom was happy to be included in the reunion. She's been curious about him, too, since I found him. Are you all up for a visit to meet the triplets? I can call Hayley to see if we can come over now."

"We'd love it!" they both said.

I stood to call Hayley. Coming back to the patio, I told them she was ready for us.

We cleared the table, closed the sliding glass door, and deposited the dishes in the sink.

Walking down the stairs, I said, "We're off on another adventure. You'll love the kids. They're almost two, getting independent and talkative. Although, they might be a little shy at first."

"We love kids. My four are sixteen, twelve, eleven, and ten. Not babies anymore. I know what it's like to have a lot of little kids around the house."

"Her kids are sweet and fun. I love being a grandmother," said Katie.

When we arrived at Hayley and Kolton's, the kids were doing chalk drawings on the driveway. They waved as we drove up.

"Gamma, Pop Pop," they yelled, as we approached them. Brent and I each picked them up and twirled them around. When they noticed Katie and Janine, they hid behind us. I introduced Katie and Janine to Hayley first. The kids were curious, peeking out around our legs.

"Kids, these are special people I want you to meet." I put one arm around Katie. "This is Katie."

She got down on her knees to their eye level.

"Hi! I'm happy to meet you. Tell me your names." The kids introduced themselves with their nicknames.

"I'm Bubba," Jax stated confidently.

"I'm Sissy," Hannah said.

"I'm K kay," little Kara announced proudly.

We all laughed. "Yes, those are the names you call each other. This is Jax, Hannah, and Kara." I pointed to each one. "And this is Janine. Katie is her mom."

"Hello. You are all cute. I like your chalk drawings."

Katie looked at the two girls. "It's going to take a while to figure out which one is Hannah, and which is Kara."

I nodded. "I'll make it easier for you. Hannah is in the pink shirt, and Kara is in purple. I do the same thing with Mom. She can't tell them apart, either. Brent and I spend a lot of time with them. We don't have trouble with it. Their personalities are different, too."

Katie turned to Hayley. "You certainly have your hands full. Three times blessed."

Hayley looked down as her three kids picked up chalk to start drawing again.

"Yes, they are both a joy and a lot of work."

"It's hot out here. Can we go inside?" I asked Hayley.

"Yes, I'm hot, too. Come on, kids. Put the chalk down for now. Let's go inside, and you can show Katie and Janine your rooms."

The three of them dropped the chalk they were holding and ran into the house. They weren't the least bit shy when it came to showing off their rooms and toys. Kara reached up with both arms to Katie, who picked her up.

Squeezing Kara, Katie said, "This is like heaven having little ones in your arms. You are precious."

We all went down the hall to Jax's room first. Right next door was the girls' room.

"They're still small for two-year-olds," Hayley commented. "We've kept them in cribs. When they're ready, the crib sides can be taken off."

"You mean when you're ready." I laughed. "No night wanderers allowed. Can you imagine all three of them coming into your room at night?"

"One more reason to keep the sides up." Hayley smiled.

We all sat on the floor in the girls' room, as they pulled out all their dolls. Jax came in with trucks and dinosaurs. The three were happy to have a new audience. Katie and Janine played along, holding the dolls or rolling the trucks along the floor.

Around four o'clock, Kolton came home. We introduced him to Katie and Janine.

"Do you want us to get pizza for dinner?" I asked. "I don't know if the kids eat it, but the adults can have it."

"I'll make mac and cheese for the kids. Yes, pizza sounds great. The kids will eat breadsticks. I'll call it in and have it delivered."

At five o'clock, we set up the folding table and chairs for the kids. The pizza was piping hot. Hayley dished up the kids' dinner and broke breadsticks for them. We each got paper plates for slices of pizza and a breadstick.

The kids didn't want to sit still and eat their dinner. Jax climbed onto Kolton's lap, Hannah raised her arms to Hayley, and Kara stood looking up at Brent.

"Try resisting that look." I laughed. "I'll get their dinner bowls and bring them over to our table. Maybe we can get them to finish it."

Brent hoisted Kara onto his lap. She watched, fascinated, as he took a bite of pizza.

"You'll like pizza when you get older," he told Kara. Looking around at the other kids, he added, "You will, too, Jax and Hannah."

The triplets played musical laps. Jumping off one lap and waiting to be lifted by the next person.

"They're too distracted to eat," Hayley said. "We can clear their stuff off the table."

We had our fill of pizza and threw our paper plates away. Katie and Janine were stifling yawns. It was time to go home and relax. Bedtime would be early tonight after an active day.

Tomorrow, we'll drive by our old house and go to Mom's condo. Maybe make a trip to Cabrillo Monument. Being a tourist in San Diego was fun. Even for those of us who live here.

CHAPTER THIRTY-FIVE

We all got up at seven and had cereal for breakfast. Mom expected us at eleven thirty.

"Would you like to see the neighborhood where we raised our kids? We can drive by there on our way to Mom's," I asked.

"Yes, we'd love to," said Janine.

At ten thirty, we climbed into the car and got on the freeway. Fifteen minutes later, we were at Scripps Ranch.

"That's Miramar Lake on the left," Brent said, pointing out his window. "It's close to our house. We used to walk from our house around the lake. It's over five miles."

We entered the development where our house had been built. I told them, "This section happened to be under construction when we were house hunting. All the homes were brand new. Some roads weren't paved yet. We saw the model and fell in love with the floor plan. That was back in 1986."

"It looks like a nice area," said Katie, looking out the car window. "I love cul-de-sacs."

Happy memories danced around in my head, and my voice thickened.

"This street turned out to be great for the kids growing up. Every-one kept an eye on the kids playing on the sidewalks. There were a group of five girls around Hayley's age who played together. Here's our old house on the right."

"You had a pretty big front yard," Janine noted. "And side yards, too."

"Yes, and a big backyard," said Brent. "We were able to add on to the entire backside of the house with an additional six hundred and sixty square feet. The entire front yard was grass, but I didn't mind mowing it."

Brent slowed down to let them have a better look at the house. We all rolled down our windows.

I sighed. "We loved it here, but with the kids on their own, we decided to downsize."

Katie looked around at the neighboring houses. "I can see why you moved here. Great space for families."

After a short tour of Scripps Ranch, we headed to Mom's condo in Pt. Loma. We found a parking place and rode the elevator to the top floor. Mom had the front door open.

"We're here," I called out.

"Come on in, everyone," she answered.

After hugging Brent and me, she turned to Katie and Janine. "I have been excited to meet you both. Patrish has waited a long time for this reunion."

Katie gave her a hug. "We're honored you invited us. I've wanted to thank you for raising her and giving her such a good home."

Janine had tears in her eyes as she hugged Mom. "Those are my sentiments, too. We've bonded with Patrish and can't imagine not having her in our lives."

Now we were all wiping away tears.

"You have to see this view," I told them, leading them out to the balcony.

Katie's breath caught. "What a beautiful view of the bay. You're up high enough to see all around San Diego."

"This is one of the perks of living on the top floor," Mom told them. "I had a condo in this building on a lower floor, but it didn't have a pretty view. We love looking out at the boats."

Brent pointed out toward the water. "On the fourth of July, you can see fireworks from every direction. We sit here on the balcony, turn on the corresponding radio station for the music, and enjoy the show."

"It sounds wonderful," Janine said. "I love the fourth of July."

I nodded. "We do, too. Summer is my favorite season."

While they were admiring the view, Mom and I went into the kitchen to get lunch ready. She had prepared chicken salad, croissants, and lemonade. We called everyone in to eat.

After saying grace, we passed the food around. Janine turned to my mom and asked, "I'm curious. What was Patrish like growing up?"

"She wanted to be the peacemaker, always trying to keep everyone from getting into trouble. Josh and Blake were only sixteen months apart in age. They wrestled and could get rowdy."

"Don't forget the moody, broody part," I added, laughing. I set down my fork. "Typical teenage girl. Only interested in myself. I doubt Blake and Josh considered me helpful. Lindsay and most of my friends were off riding their horses. I didn't ride, so I spent many hours alone."

Brent furrowed his eyebrows. "Don't feel sorry for her, though. They had a big house, several acres, a horse corral, swimming pool, and paddle tennis court." He took a bite of chicken salad.

"Boy, no crying for you," Katie joked, popping a piece of croissant in her mouth.

"I know how good I had it. Well, as I got older, I figured it out. Mom and Dad tried to keep us grounded."

Mom looked over at Katie. "Where did you grow up?"

"We lived in Texas during my high school years. I almost came to San Diego to go to United States International University in my junior year. I would've received college credits for it. I decided not to go there. I spent a lot of my summers with my grandparents in Newport Beach. I love California."

"I was raised in Yucaipa. I ended up in Georgia after the Army," Janine added.

After taking a sip of lemonade, Mom said, "That must have been quite an adventure. I'm glad you stayed safe."

"I did everything I could to talk her out of going into the Army. I even made her watch the movie *Private Benjamin,* hoping she'd see what a big commitment it would be. She has a mind of her own. The movie didn't deter her one bit," said Katie.

Brent said to Mom, "This chicken salad is excellent. A perfect summer meal."

"Yes, Mom, thank you."

Mom stood. "Is everyone finished eating? We have lemon cake for dessert since Patrish doesn't eat chocolate."

Katie's mouth opened in surprise. "You don't eat chocolate? Don't you like it, or are you allergic to it?"

"I'm a bona fide chocoholic. Can't get enough of it. No matter how much I ate, I never got sick. But I gained weight." I stood to help clear the table.

Janine got up to help me. "If you're a chocoholic, how did you stop eating it?"

Brent and Mom had heard the story at least one hundred times. They both grinned.

"One day at work, we were eating Peanut M&M's. One of the staff commented she hadn't had any chocolate today and didn't want to indulge. I tried to think of a day, any day, I'd resisted it. I decided the next day to stand up against temptation. One day led to the next, and before I knew it, I was chocolate free, but it didn't come easy. I had an addiction to chocolate. Poor Brent. The first few years he couldn't eat it around me, and I wouldn't let him have any in our home. I've gone thirty-three years now."

"I'm glad she never made me quit, too," Brent said, laughing. "I love it, but only eat one piece at a time."

I grimaced. "I could make a short order of a one-pound box of See's candies. One piece only made me want more. It's embarrassing. I'll never go back to that bad habit."

Setting down a piece of cake in front of Katie, Janine asked, "What do you do when you're over at someone's house and the dessert is chocolate? It seems to be the favorite flavor for everyone."

"You're right. Most people serve it. I don't mind when it turns out to be the dessert. I say a polite 'no thank you.' Most of my friends know not to serve it. I don't always have to eat dessert. I'm the crazy one, not them. It's a decision I made."

We stopped chatting for a few minutes, enjoying the lemon cake. Katie and Brent cleared the dishes, and we went into the living room to relax. Mom asked Katie many of the same questions I had asked about Nora—what was she like, and what Katie's childhood memories were of her. We were running out of things to talk about, and it was time to say goodbye to Mom.

On the car ride home, Katie leaned forward in her seat. "Your mom is wonderful. So nice and friendly. I can see why you speak highly of her."

I turned to face her. "Mom is great. I have always admired her. Janine, you know having four kids is hard work. We all had different personalities. Couldn't have been easy."

Janine smiled. "It keeps me hopping. There's six years from oldest to youngest. We're always busy."

"We were close in age, too. Seven years from oldest to youngest. It makes me tired thinking about it." I laughed.

"It's hard to believe you guys are leaving tomorrow," said Brent. "We're glad you both decided to come out here."

"We were ready to make the connection in 2005. I wish we could have. But things work out for a reason. Mom couldn't handle it, I guess." Katie shrugged her shoulders.

I sighed. "Now we have each other. This bond will never be broken. Let's get back to our condo. Your plane leaves early tomorrow.

We can watch one of our favorite Christian movies, *Courageous.*"

Brent grilled hamburgers out on the patio for dinner. We had a quiet evening laughing and watching the movie. It was early to bed.

The next morning, there were long hugs at the airport. Tears glistened in our eyes. We promised to stay in touch and keep sending pictures. What a blessing to have found Katie and Janine.

CHAPTER THIRTY-SIX

SEPTEMBER 14, 2019

Laughter filled the room, bouncing off the walls. Bright orange, yellow, purple, and blue table clothes covered the tables. Streamers hung over the two doors. Balloons were tied to the back of chairs, while others were bunched together in a bouquet.

Heads turned at the squeals from Hannah, Jax, Kara, and Alex. They raced around the room brandishing balloons, shouting, "Look at us, Gigi." Their cousin, Paxton, followed in close pursuit, roaring. My brother, Josh, laughed, sitting with his family next to Mom at the table.

"There you go, Gigi, your first round of entertainment," he said to Mom.

Mom watched her great-grandchildren. "Was that an actual roar? Paxton's playing the role to the hilt."

"Happy birthday, Grandma!" our family of seven from Hawaii shouted as they entered the room.

"We're so happy you're here." I stood and clapped.

"Celebrating a ninety-first birthday is a big deal," Ren said, walking over to Mom. "We wouldn't miss it for anything. We love you, Grandma." She stood, and he enveloped her in a big hug.

The rest of the Hawaii group took turns hugging and kissing her. We all rushed toward them to get our hugs.

I was so happy. "It's been a while since we were all together. This is going to be a day to remember," I said.

I clasped my hands in front of my chest. Our whole family was together to celebrate. We had travelers from Colorado, Arizona, Pennsylvania, Hawaii, as well as our hometown of San Diego. Mom's three children were here, eight grandchildren, and nine great-grandchildren. Including spouses, our total came to thirty.

"Now that we have everyone here, let's take pictures," my sister Lindsay called out. "Josh, gather your family around Mom. Okay, scoot in. We want to get all nine of you in the shot. Good."

Cameras flashed all around the room.

"Ren, you guys are next. Say cheese!" Lindsay clicked the camera. We all followed suit.

"Patrish, we'll get your whole family in. This is a big group. Put the great-grandkids on either side of Mom's chair. The rest of you squish in. Say happy birthday. That's a great shot."

"Next up, Lindsay and Matt. This will be easy, compared to the big groups. Got it," I said.

The room we had rented at Mom's condo for the party had a kitchen. Hayley and I set about preparing the appetizers, veggie trays, cheese, salami and crackers, mini quiches, chips, and dip. We set them on the table with the purple tablecloth, along with napkins and paper plates.

I watched Mom as each family member took the time to sit and talk to her. Her smile said it all. This was her family. The people she cared about and would fiercely defend and love forever. I caught her eye and blew her a kiss. It had proved to be difficult to get us all together through the years. Busy lives, distant locations, but no one wanted to miss a chance to celebrate Mom's birthday this year. God's rich blessings abounded.

I thought back to the videos Amanda gave me of the Donovan gatherings. Family love, that's what it's all about. Being with the ones you cherished. Laughter, loving, celebrating all life has to offer. I'd missed the occasions the Donovans shared, but not those with this wonderful family I grew up with. Did we get along all the time? No. Misunderstandings, vying for attention, *that's not fair*, are a part of most families.

I wish Blake could've been here for this celebration today. His side of the family lived in Hawaii and made up seven of our clan. We'd also lost his daughter, Rita, in a car accident in 2006. Every family has their struggles.

After most of the appetizers were consumed, Hayley and I cleared the tables and brought out the birthday cake. I set a large chocolate sheet cake, brightly decorated with icing flowers and *HAPPY BIRTHDAY,* in front of Mom. We sang our off-key version of the beloved birthday song and cheered her on as she blew out the candles.

"At least you didn't try to put ninety-one candles on the cake." She laughed. "We would've started a fire."

I cut the cake and gave her the first piece. Lindsay distributed cake to everyone, and Josh cleared his throat and raised his cup.

"I'd like to propose a toast. Here's to Mom. We love you and are happy to be together celebrating your special day."

Everyone chimed in, "To Mom. We love you."

Chatter broke out as the cake was consumed and family members continued to catch up on each other's lives. I glanced over at my kids. Hayley and Kolton were supervising the triplets as they ate their cake. Not every bite made it into their mouths. Nate and Anna laughed with Alex. Brent was recovering from a hard year of fighting cancer. His joyful expression showed how much he valued life. My heart was full.

After Mom finished eating her cake, Josh brought over the birthday cards and small gifts, placing them in front of her. Tears welled in Mom's eyes as she read the cards. She beamed while opening a collection of picture frames, a desk calendar, and a copy of *The Noel Stranger* by Richard Paul Evans. Lindsay placed a purple orchid plant from her and Matt on the table.

"Now you have frames for all the great pictures we took today. I expect to see them displayed next time we come over." Josh chuckled.

"Thank you all so much. I love each and every one of you. These orchids are beautiful. This has been a wonderful birthday."

A smile lit up my face. God has always been faithful during this journey. I didn't know where it would lead when it first began. My heart had been hopeful, broken, and restored. I learned a lot about myself, God, and the importance of family.

I'm forever grateful for finding my biological family. They hold a special place in my heart. I've remained close to Katie, Amanda, and Janine. Their welcoming arms opened a new world for me. I understand the reluctance of some members of the family. Our worlds were far apart.

Ron and I kept in touch for a little while. He, too, will always have a piece of my heart. It's a comfort to know my *first* family is out there. We may not see each other often, but I know they are there.

I've heard it said that life is like a tapestry. We look up and see the messy underside, threads hanging down, random colors mixed with no pattern. It looks like a jumble from our view. God sees the masterpiece from the top. Each stitch He placed in a specific spot. Intertwining lives, beauty, rich colors. All His doing. His design. Full of purpose.

This wonderful, lively, sometimes nutty family I had gathered with to celebrate Mom's birthday was the backbone of who I had become. Every single one of them has influenced my life. It had been God's plan from the beginning to place me where I needed to be. My spot in the tapestry.

Over my desk I have a paraphrase wall hanging of Jeremiah 29:11

On the journey
God will….
Save and protect you.
Lead and direct your steps.
Give wisdom.
Fill you with hope.
Strengthen with power.
Bless you with good things.
Be faithful to the end.

This journey had indeed been ordained. Family means *everything*

THE END

ACKNOWLEDGMENTS

Writing this book has taken me on a fantastic journey and learning experience. I want to thank my husband, Bill, for his never-ending support, love and encouragement. To my children, Heather and Nick, thank you for cheering me on, especially when I got discouraged. Always, a thank you to my mom, Leila Champ. You have helped me become the person I am today.

A very special thanks to the team at Author Ready, under the guidance and mentorship of Richard Paul Evans. My story came to life with the help I received at every turn. Thank you to Debbie Ihler Rasmussen for your input and direction as my content editor. Kirsten Capunay for my beautiful cover. Kim Autrey patiently went through my manuscript as a copy editor, fine tuning the story. Francine Platt put it all together professionally as my formatter. Thank you, Richard, for your friendship and the opportunities you give to writers.

Thank you to my dear friend, Cynthia Gustafson, who kept me believing I could accomplish my dream of writing a book. Thank you to my "first" family I discovered when I completed my own adoption search. Andrea Clancy, you and your family welcomed me with open arms. Karen Costa and Jen Hutchinson, I am so happy to have you in my life.

Writing might be a solitary pursuit, but I was surrounded by love and friendship. Thank you to everyone who helped me along the way.

Printed in the USA
CPSIA information can be obtained
at www.ICGtesting.com
JSHW021733030823
45858JS00001B/56